The Ice Dancer

by Konnie Ellis

This book is a work of fiction. Any resemblance to actual events or persons, living or dead, is entirely coincidental.

Cover photo by Lane Ellis.

"The Ice Dancer," by Konnie Ellis. ISBN 978-1-60264-580-6 (softcover); 978-1-60264-581-3 (ebook).

Published 2010 by Virtualbookworm.com Publishing Inc., P.O. Box 9949, College Station, TX 77842, US.

For Lilly, in her 92nd year,
and Bob, Lane, Julie,
Erik, Lynn and Mehana

PART 1

Chapter 1
New York City

Greta prances down the subway stairs, rushing to catch up. The momentum and rhythm of her steps speeds her down the stairwell to the clatter of her own footsteps–so loud, so noticeable, as she descends. Where is everyone? Where's Gabriel? She continues down the stairs to the echoey clacking of her shoes against the stairs–a lilting rhythmic patter against cement steps, but now with little halts, bits of doubt; questions reverberating under the high ceiling of the station. She takes the last few steps, and stops. Because it's dark. Because it's late–too late for young girls to be traipsing down dark empty subway tunnels.

She took a wrong turn. She shouldn't have taken these stairs–this is not the right place at all. No train is coming here. She is completely alone. But wait–there are shapes in the dark–the dark shapes of men. She catches her breath. Five, maybe six–a half-dozen troll men, all around her in the dark. Their shadows move with them, toward her. They move like slime–steady, quiet, surrounding her–big-shouldered shadow men from the subway tunnel, shaggy hair like weeds gone to seed, beards of hay. The smell of earth, of goats; foul breath. Close, too close, these ghouls of the night with eyes like owls.

Run. That's all she can think–just run fast. Jump. Up the stairs. Don't fall, don't stumble, just keep going. Don't freeze. Her heart pounds, her legs are rubbery, yet she leaps, almost dives upward through the air, taking three stairs at a time. Her lungs are on fire and she gasps for breath as she reaches the top of the stairs, nearly breathless, near tears; flying. Into Gabriel's arms.

"Greta."

"Gabriel, oh Gabriel." she whispers. She can't stop shaking. He holds her, wipes the sweat from her forehead, strokes her hair, until her heart returns to normal. They walk toward the light to join the other dancers, waiting in their little group, jabbering, sipping Evian.

———————

Greta falls asleep as soon as the plane leaves La Guardia. Gabriel is asleep in the window seat beside her when she wakes. The flight attendant smiles kindly and Greta accepts a fuzzy wool blanket. She wants to wake Gabriel. She needs to talk and wants him to understand, but she lets him sleep, tucks the blanket around herself, and slips off her shoes. How did she do that? So foolish. To come out of the ladies room at Penn Station, get turned around like that, worried they would all be waiting for her and so rush off in the wrong direction. It was the excitement and the confusion of the station, and the exhilaration of being in New York City and seeing Gabriel dance. It was the first time she had seen him dance professionally. It seemed amazing, yet natural considering his talent; that he would be dancing in New York while still a student. Of course she had seen him dance all year at school performances, and she knew he had danced in New York before, even Paris. She knew all this, but still this trip to New York made her giddy, out of control. Her spine tingled, remembering the concert hall and Gabriel leaping across the stage. But the bad part she wants to forget–how she had run down those steps to the mole people; potato people–the sooty yellow lights of the subway glazing their skin a ghoulish green. Greta pictures the subway men hunched together for a group photo for a horror movie; grinning their ghoulish grins, their potato flesh made up like green-skinned trolls. Yes, think of them as actors, not real men who actually live in the subway, and were about to.... Greta pulls the blanket tight across her shoulders, hugging herself. *Just men gone mad, gone hungry, that's all.*

She closes her eyes, grateful, so grateful for her escape. She got away. But now she'll have to pay, won't she? Pay for getting away, for being so foolish, for being the youngest dancer in the troupe–chosen by Gabriel as his dance partner, his friend–the other dancers so jealous, always waiting for her to make a mistake. But they were nice. They were concerned–glad to see her. So tired. Exhausted. Her mind jumps with a confusion of trolls and dancers and the recirculated air of the plane laced with de-icer, plastic, and old coffee, mingling and settling into one substantial headache. Greta moans softly to herself. Gabriel reaches over and takes her hand.

Chapter 2
Greta in Canada

Five years have passed and Gabriel is dead. Someone told her so. But is it true? Does she dare find out? These crazy dreams are driving her crazy. Another one last night...

It's cold. Greta watches the smoky figure of Gabriel's ghost on the shore through her own icy breath. He turns and walks into the water, into the silky moonlight on the surface of the lake. She listens to the quiet lapping of waves against his thighs. He walks further and further out along the shallow sandbar toward the center of the lake, until he becomes a sleek black horse with a blue-black mane and sky blue wings. She's not surprised by his turning into a winged horse, and watches the apparition flap its wings and rise above the water, flying slowly and gracefully up into the night sky until she is alone beneath a sky filled with countless stars.

Greta returns to the fire and warms her icy hands before she walks from fire to fire to greet her friends, out so late at night, waiting too, in their dreams.

She doesn't mind the dreams, after all, they're just dreams. It's really the daytime she's concerned about. For a week now, she's had the sensation of being followed. This morning, for instance, it seemed someone was in the back seat of her car while she drove into town to pick up a package at the post office. And later, when she stood in the checkout line at the library and paused to glance at her watch, she sensed a presence beside her, trying to see the time on her watch. Was it Gabriel? Gabriel's ghost, spirit;

ethereal presence? Was she going crazy? It felt like it was Gabriel. Why was she listening so carefully, as if he were about to whisper in her ear? And what about last night, when she was reading in bed–hadn't something urged her to wait to turn a page until he had finished reading? Or had she just been tired, and dozing between the lines?

This afternoon she is sorting stacks of old papers and magazines in an attempt to throw out some of the clutter. She really has no reason to keep the outdated ballet magazines. She subscribed the year after she moved to Red Otter, not quite having let go of her past life.

The last time she actually saw Gabriel was in the hospital after she shattered her knee, a month after New York. She winces, recalling those days in the hospital, and the pain of her wrecked life. How sweet Gabriel had been, coming every day, bringing her a rose or a handful of wild flowers picked from behind the school–daisies and Queen Anne's Lace, or a half dozen brown-eyed susans. He would sit on the chair beside her bed and listen to whatever she wanted to talk about, and then he would tell stories; fascinating stories. He said they were just stories he made up, but they seemed so real and she loved to listen, though she sometimes drifted in and out of sleep. Then one day he touched her toes, gently, each toe of the foot in the casted leg, and then he paused, as if ready to say something important, but instead just looked at her and said nothing. After he left that day she kept seeing his face with that expression. And all that night she thought of his eyes and his silence and by morning she had decided to go away. It was true they could still be friends, but she could no longer dance. Not dancing was too much; too sad. It was pity she had seen in his eyes that she couldn't face again. Not from Gabriel.

As soon as she was released from the hospital Greta left by train, choosing a town at random from the station list, a name she'd never even heard of; Red Otter. She bought a ticket, got on the train and sat down, not so much ready to go on to a new life as to leave the old one behind. The train raced north into the forest and away from her life as a dancer, leaving Gabriel behind without a partner. Leaving herself without a friend.

She tosses the ballet magazines into a cardboard box, then, feeling guilty, like she is throwing Gabriel away, she retrieves three magazines and hugs them to her chest, and realizes she's blushing. All these years later she's blushing as though she had just left Winnipeg an hour ago, rather than five years past.

She never talks about her past. She always leaves it vague; unable to tell even her best friends about Gabriel, and how she left Winnipeg without a word to anyone. She was never good at forgiving herself. The only way she can deal with her flight is to concede that she was young. Just seventeen. She was young and smart; otherwise they would have found her. Someone would have. She sighs, sorry that she wasn't found, but still she wouldn't want to know how hard they'd tried. She's sure Gabriel tried to find her, tried very hard, even though he was in Copenhagen when she left the hospital, and Paris after that. And of course she changed her name–how *could* anyone find her? As soon as the train pulled out of the station she became Greta Winters.

On the train she sat beside an old woman named Leena, and it was this stranger, Leena, whom she told her new name. It felt good too, saying the name–Greta Winters. Yes, now she was Greta Winters. Greta smiles, remembering the hardtack Leena shared with her–a home-made rye cracker big as a plate and aptly named. Greta crunched and chewed and christened herself into a new person. Greta Winters. Greta LaJeune, the dancer, no longer existed.

Greta had shown Leena her knee, pulling her skirt up to reveal the scar with its feathery incision tracings fanning out like stars. Leena grimaced and told Greta she had spiders too. After looking up and down the aisle of the train, Leena pulled down a thick gun-metal gray stocking and showed Greta a small scar on her ankle, which she tapped, pointing out how you can see the "spiders" just under the surface of the skin. After they rearranged themselves, they sat back and finished the hardtack in silence. They both looked out the windows for the rest of the train ride, but now comfortably so. Occasionally Leena would smile in a kindly manner, as if to say, "yes, we two have spiders, and isn't it bad and isn't it nice too, the two of us like that, here on the train with our spiders." Even now she sometimes remembers Leena when she looks at the scar on her knee.

Greta reshuffles the magazines, saving the ones with her favorite pictures–Gabriel's picture is in several of the magazines–she knows the issues well. It was late fall when she left the hospital. In the hospital there were no seasons. On the train the bright colors of fall were dazzling. Greta watched mile after mile of trees as the train rolled along: bright maples and oaks, and stands of white birch, all measuring the miles like second hands on a clock. A child behind her mimicked the sound of the train softly to himself, a jazzy little phrase, ajugga, jugga, ajuggajugga. Lulled by the repetitious rhythms of the train and the endless trees, she stared out the window, conscious that she was moving toward the new. Toward a new home? The ballet school had been her home, her family, and Gabriel–she had been his partner; he had chosen her. She had it made, everyone said. She had a future.

She had a headache on the train. The buzzing and humming of the train and her headache had seemed like one, like a train in her head, until the headache started to fade with the miles. The further north she traveled the more it faded, and the better she felt. It was as if North itself was the healer; a home toward which she traveled like a homing pigeon. Rubbing her head, and repositioning herself against the seat back, she thought of Gabriel and the horrendous headaches he used to get. Migraines. He would know ahead of time by flashes of light that came before the constrictions that signaled the start of a migraine. Doctors couldn't help him; all he could do was suffer. It was hard to watch; hard to be around him during those episodes. They were all so young, and they adored Gabriel, especially the girls. West Birch School of Dance was the best ballet school in the country, and Gabriel was its star. Even the teachers were in awe of Gabriel, though they didn't show it like the students did. They all did what they could for him, which was very little.

If he had one of his headaches during class or rehearsal, he went off to the side of the tent, or to the back of the hall. Once he sat down and howled, actually howled. It was a low animal moan, and then he more or less collapsed, resting his head in his arms on the back of a chair. No one said a word, which Greta thought made it seem worse. They finished the last five minutes of class, going through their routines like robots, and afterward Mary Lou started giggling as she laced her boots, and then she hid her face in her hands and started sobbing loudly like her heart had been broken. She was the newest member of the class, and she acted out how Greta felt. One of the guys said the devil was punishing Gabriel. Who did he think he was anyway? A gazelle? But he was just jealous. Still, if Gabriel was on stage, he never let the headaches stop him. Everyone said he was a trooper.

———

Greta's legs are numb from sitting in one position for too long. Too much remembering. She feels shivery as she gets up. Again, that feeling of Gabriel being in the room with her. *Probably I'm going crazy. Why is he following me? Was he only able to find me as a ghost? Maybe I am going crazy.* Greta shrugs and almost laughs. If she has to have a ghost following her around, looking at her watch, resting in the back seat of her car, turning up right here in her house, she would just as soon it be Gabriel. Of course, she'd rather he were alive. Looking out toward the lake she admires the pale orange late afternoon sky.

Pausing at the table she studies a drawing of a swan. She knows she's changing. She can see it in her embroidery designs. Each week she sends off one or two new cross-stitch or embroidery designs to the publisher in Winnipeg. She makes good money selling the designs, which are mass produced and sold in kits all over Canada and in the States, but her new love is stained glass. Just this last week she worked from the swan drawing, creating a round wall hanging of the graceful swan on a glassy lake of blue, with a purple and violet sky, bordered by bare black trees. It doesn't have anything to do with ballet, or with Gabriel, she's pretty sure.

Greta stores the piles of magazines in the hall closet and dumps the few items she's managed to toss out into the trash bin. Tonight is a skating night. By late November the lake has frozen over and her neighbor, Karloff, has cleared a portion of the lake by his dock for a rink and moved his old ice house into a corner for changing from boots into skates. His dock light is bright enough to light most of the rink at night, which is when they skate. It was Gabriel who showed Greta how to lace her ballet slippers, taught her how to tighten them gradually, to grip both edges firmly with one hand, and hold her foot just right–not too stiff yet not too relaxed, as she finished the lacing. She thinks of her slippers every time she laces her skates.

Tonight Karloff is skating slowly around the rink in

his lumbering but elegant manner, hunched slightly forward in a great black coat, his long arms swaying back and forth rhythmically; right, left, right, left. His heavy dark pants are bunched up above his gray wool socks, and it's hard to tell where his black cassock hat ends and his thick grisly beard begins. Their mutual neighbor, Latos, calls Karloff *Bearloff,* or just Bear. Long ago, in Winnipeg, and long before Greta was a ballet student, Karloff was a hockey player. Now, like Greta, Karloff relives his past on the rink. Two nights a week after the rink is readied, each Tuesday and Saturday night, unless the temperature dips below -20°, they skate, silently gliding around the rink in circle after circle. They never talk while they skate. Sometimes the howl of a wolf from the other side of the frozen lake lingers over the silence of their cold spot-lit rink. Otherwise the only sound is the rhythmic glitch, glatch of the metal skate blades on hard ice, punctuated at regular intervals by Greta's quick cutting turns that scar the ice, and if her knee isn't bothering her and she is in an exuberant mood, an occasional clattery spin.

Karloff keeps a coffee can full of hockey pucks in the ice house, and a couple of hockey sticks in the corner which appear to be made entirely of black tape. But he never uses them when Greta skates with him, they just skate in circles. Tonight is Saturday night, and Greta and Karloff have taken off their skates in the ice house and walked the short stretch up the hill to Karloff's cabin. The moon is nearly full, making the snowy path bright and the white birch trees particularly noticeable. As usual, Greta hangs her skates on a nail on Karloff's porch for next time. Her white wool socks dangle out of the skates above a big sack of dog food.

"You ought to give someone that dog food," she tells Karloff as she leaves the porch.

"Yah, I suppose," he says, but knows he won't. He'll

just let it get stale. Bandit has been dead now nearly six months, and the near-full sack of dog food sitting on the porch next to the stacks of newspapers is a comfort to him.

"See you at Latos's," Greta shouts out through the cold as she heads down the driveway past Karloff's old pickup.

Karloff waves and says nothing, but stands to watch her walk to her car to see if it starts okay. The Volvo starts readily, and Greta is glad she had the tune-up in town Friday and put in high octane gas. By the time she took off her skates she could tell without a thermometer that it was already well below zero, probably -15°, at least. Greta drives straight to the lodge. She, Karloff and the other permanent residents who have houses on this side of the lake go over to Latos Lodge each Saturday night. Saturday night is sauna night. Greta has been honoring this Saturday sauna ritual for four years now, starting the second year she moved to the lake.

Walking to the sauna she can smell the smoky birch fire that Latos prepared earlier in the day, as he does each Saturday. Up here, families sauna together and parents and children are comfortable with a healthy, robust nudity, but the unrelated groups at Latos Lodge split up among the sexes, with the women going first and the men afterward. In summer people swim in the warmish water of the lake after the sauna, and in winter, a few of the old-timers enjoy an invigorating roll in the snow.

Greta likes sitting on the warm, steamy wooden shelves with the other women. She finds it a comfortable, primitive situation unlike anything she's known, and she likes being part of this group of women so unlike herself in many ways, but still like herself in some basic way. She is relaxed here as she is nowhere else, and likes this older and simpler way of life. In the sauna they talk a little, joke a little, but mostly just sit and enjoy the sauna–its unique woody incense, the pleasant damp cedar boards beneath them, and the heavy moist air. Here they share a human warmth which seems animal-like to Greta, like foxes in a den.

Later, back in the lodge, they are refreshed and hungry again, even though most everyone came early and already had venison stew and cornbread before sitting in the sauna. The women take off their boots and settle into easy chairs around the big stone fireplace. Millie, the twin with nine toes, brings a bottle of Moosehead beer and a glass to each of the five women, and places a big bowl of peanuts on the small wooden table near the fire. She sets aside a second bowl for the men, who are having their turn in the sauna.

Sipping beer, they catch up on the events of the week. Tillie and Millie thawed blueberries and baked fifteen blueberry pies for their church bizarre. Mable canned a dozen quart jars of venison stew, and a half dozen pints of partridge. She uses lemon rind with the venison, plus carrots, onions and potatoes, and bay leaf in both the stews. And Faun is nearly done with her fall weaving for a shop down in Thunder Bay. Greta tells about her swan stained-glass window, while thinking it would be nice to make small stained-glass window hangings for all of her sauna friends this year, though she knows there isn't enough time, she would have had to have started last summer, in August at the latest. Tonight, resting quietly in front of the fire in stockinged feet, before the men return from the sauna, the women are content, relaxed from the steam and the beer, and another simple, productive week. Greta feels at ease for the first time all week, and is thinking of telling them how Gabriel has been visiting her from beyond the grave. Mable often speaks of her weekly visit to the town cemetery to talk things over with her beloved Johnny. But then she hears the sauna door slam and decides maybe next week, if Gabriel isn't gone by then, and besides, she could use more time.

The men are talking quietly as they enter the lodge, their faces red and shiny from the sauna. They open their beers at the bar, except Otto, who no longer drinks and settles for a root beer. At nine o'clock, the bird in the cuckoo clock begins to count out the hours, and they are all settled in their chairs by the time the crooked little man with the cane and the bent women with a cat in a basket come out from the wooden clock door and move jerkily around to a second door, which closes neatly behind them.

In the summer Latos plays the piano on sauna nights, but hardly ever in winter, except at Christmas. He says his hands get too cold and stiff in winter weather, so they sit and drink and talk a little, not much, unless someone has a story. Mainly they sit and look at the fire, which crackles and flickers its light over the gold logs of the lodge room and over the bear and timber wolf skins tacked to the walls. At nine thirty, though later in summer, Latos plugs in the jukebox and plays a song to end the evening– usually the *Tennessee Waltz*, but sometimes, *What'll I Do*, or a Swedish waltz that's been on the jukebox ever since Greta started coming to the sauna evenings. It was Faun who first invited her. The rest of the songs on the jukebox are current popular songs left over from the previous summer when the lodge is open for dinner until eight o'clock and the bar stays open until eleven on weekends.

On the way to the car they pass Latos's husky team in their kennel. A few of the dogs are awake and pace back and forth. Shadow, who is half wolf and half Siberian Husky, and the only pup to survive from last spring's litter, stops to watch as they pass by. He has one blue eye and one yellow-brown eye, a white masked face and a heavy black body with a wolf's lanky legs. Last week Shadow followed Faun and Greta down to their cars and nudged Greta hard. She had nearly fallen in her rush to get away from the dog and into her car, though she's known Shadow since he was a few weeks old. He was one of the pups Latos let wander around, and he still roams around on his own most of the time, as he did last week.

Greta finds herself wondering if Latos keeps Shadow in the pen with the others during a full moon, and is surprised at the spooky feeling she has tonight. She's never paid much attention to Shadow before—before this past week anyway. In winter the dogs take on a wildness you don't notice so much in summer, which makes her wonder just how wild they really are, just what they might do, and particularly Shadow. When Faun says his eyes are half wolf and half human, Greta is silent, but she thinks about Shadow as she drives home that night.

Chapter 3
Gabriel in Canada

The telephone rings as Gabriel pulls an Icelandic jacket over his head. He lets the door slam behind him as he strides down the snowy backyard path to the orchard. He pauses to look at the raspberry patch, where the tallest canes poke out of a snowdrift, and he makes a mental note to thaw some berries from the freezer for later. This year was his best crop, and many days he sat out under the apple trees eating big bowls of berries with thick cream; so sweet, so delicious. A few frozen berries in the snow catch his attention, their red startling against the fresh white snow, and somehow disturbing, yet beautiful too. He fills the bird feeder in the orchard, then sits for a moment on the old wooden bench where it faces the winter sun. When he can't get to the lake, this is where he comes, to his trees, his orchard: six Canadian MacIntoshes, three Wealthies, two Northern Spy, and one struggling Golden Delicious. Here in the orchard he feels at home, and happy. Almost happy. A few apples still hang in the highest branches. He counts ten, then watches a crow land on the back fence. The phone ringing in the distance breaks his meditation. The same caller? He gets up abruptly and heads toward the house, aware that he is walking out of a winter scene like one might step right out of a painting–leaving behind a bare spot in the landscape. The migraine he tried to shake in the orchard creeps back into his brow like a heavy numbing slug, yet he laughs and stretches his arms in the crisp winter air toward the sky.

Gabriel sits in Dr. Saunier's waiting room and leafs through a travel magazine. He studies a photo of a couple drinking wine on a picturesque balcony in Tuscany. He knows the wine on their table from its label, and he recognizes the model, Nichole, from his days with the Paris Ballet. For a time she was the girlfriend of a friend, and he wasn't very fond of her, though he loved to watch her walk. She walked like an African woman balancing a jug of water on her head–erect, elegant, a female cat. She was French-Haitian. She was gorgeous.

"Gabriel, how are you?" Dr. Saunier asks warmly, welcoming him to his acupuncture session.

After a lifetime of tortuous migraines, Gabriel is grateful to begin a second week without pain. Dr. Saunier's needles have given him the relief he never thought possible, and he doesn't mind the odd side effects, such as last Wednesday when he was so energized after Dr. Saunier worked on his neck that he couldn't sleep for three days, yet felt no fatigue whatsoever. Living without the migraines makes him feel like a new person, which indeed he really believes he is. He shaved his beard of five years, and has an optimism he hasn't had for years.

Funny, when he shaved his beard, as he rinsed out the sink, he thought of Greta. She was the one who told him to grow a beard. She said people will tell you their secrets if you grow a beard. And he had laughed, naturally. Ballet dancers never have beards. Odd how she knew though. She was barely 16; he was 18. So the beard was a very deliberate act on his part, marking his transition from performer to teacher at the age of 23.

He still has daydreams about Greta. And sometimes he dreams of her at night. After she left, he could never find her. He was in Europe when she got out of the hospital. She had injured her knee in an unlucky fall on icy stairs after an early storm–an ugly twist to her right knee. When he returned she was gone and that was the last he heard of her. Zapped, as if into thin air. But he knew she must be somewhere, somewhere in Canada's vast white expanse of ice and snow. Frozen alive, sometimes he thought that, when he had bad dreams. So many lost frozen souls in Canada, his Canada, his dancing home, the land of frozen calves and thighs and legs of glass. In Italy, Gabriel had actually started to thaw. He was limber, he went to discos, his migraines were less frequent, though more severe, or he might still be there.

Now, lying on his stomach on the acupuncture table listening to Dr. Saunier's water fountain, those summertime days with Greta seem as distant as a dream but pleasant to remember while he's stretched out like this. He can almost hear the water bubbling along in the stream they used to follow behind the school on the way to the park. And the birds. He loved the birds chattering as they strolled along the path beside the river. It wasn't exactly strolling but more like they were walking and floating at the same time, moving along like some sort of watery birds. Sometimes he and Greta held hands, when Violet wasn't along. Violet joined them occasionally and he didn't mind because Greta seemed more at ease with the three of them, at least at first. Later they would leave before Violet could join them, walking quickly away from the school. Then they got into the habit of having picnics in the park. Greta made sandwiches of radishes or cottage cheese and cucumbers. Sometimes Swiss cheese on rye. She was inventive. And apples. He brought the apples. And he kept wanting to kiss Greta, especially after the apples. He always wanted to but she seemed so young. Was he waiting for her to grow up? Had he wanted her to remain innocent a while longer? And then when he was sure they were both ready, the first snow fell and ended the privacy of the picnics, plus new rehearsal schedules and his travels limited their time together.

He sighs and wiggles his toes. He knows Dr. Saunier is nearly finished because he has the Lilliputian sensation he gets toward the end. He feels big and loose and weightless, as if he could float in space if the table were slipped out from under him. Comfortable within his body, and with his closed eyes, he thinks of ancestral wings resting lightly on his shoulder blades. Before he gets up, Dr. Saunier moves him near the sink and pours the warm scented oil over his forehead. The oil smells like forests and exotic gardens. This anointing with oil is his favorite part, though Dr. Saunier tells him it's not traditional to acupuncture, but he likes to incorporate various Eastern procedures for his patients, as needed, and they all seem to enjoy the scented oil. His assistant, Trina, washes Gabriel's hair in tea tree oil shampoo, and as she rinses his hair, with his eyes closed, he thinks of himself under a warm tropical waterfall. She dries his hair and combs it into place, and aware of Trina's smile floating around the room under the cloud of her hair, he slips on his coat and drifts out of the office with his next appointment card in his hand.

Chapter 4

Faun and Greta are on their way to Thunder Bay. Greta has a box of stained-glass work in the fleece-lined trunk of Faun's Ford, and Faun's recent weavings are piled loosely on the back seat. They plan to drop off their work at the craft cooperative near the knitting shop, and then have lunch.

It started snowing around dawn, just after they left the lake, and has been snowing lightly all morning. Faun's car is white, so looking out the window they see only the bright white of the Canadian winter. Faun is driving and Greta keeps dozing off. She hasn't been sleeping well. When she is awake she watches the road and pictures herself and Faun as little figurines in a glass paperweight snow scene, but the snow never settles to the bottom, it just keeps snowing and snowing. The night of the last sauna she dreamed of animals, of the wolf and bear skins on the walls of the lodge swelling up and filling their empty skins so that the entire wall seemed alive. There were too many eyes, and the mouths moved about like centipedes made of teeth. Every night since, she has had a nightmare she can't remember during the day, but she wakes suddenly afterward and knows it was a nightmare and her nightgown is soaked with sweat. Last night she thought she saw eyes on the other side of the frosty window of her bedroom before she fell asleep, and again when she awoke in the middle of the night. She plans to look for sleeping pills in Thunder Bay.

The snow continues to fall, and it remains just bright enough to see a slight shadow at the edge of the road indicating the ditch. Faun says it's more like flying an airplane in the clouds than driving a car on a road.

"It's dream-like, isn't it?" Faun says, partly to see if Greta is awake.

"I wish I had such dreams," she says. "I've been having bad dreams lately."

Faun looks over at Greta, who looks sad and doesn't elaborate so she drives on in silence. Several miles later Greta tells Faun that she has always loved the snow, that she and her friends used to make snow angels on winter nights, then just lie there in the snow looking up at the stars, cozy in their snowsuits and thick woolen mittens. She remembers the feel of lint against her tongue from her wool scarf, and how warm her scarf was, even though it was wet from her breath. They were just kids and naturally high on the simple wonders of the world.

"I'd like to die like that," Greta says.

"You scare me today," Faun says, startled at Greta's comment. But Greta laughs, and tells her she's just thinking of the perfection of those winter nights, lying in the snow.

"Come on now, surely you've had moments so perfect you could happily die in them, no?" she asks Faun.

Feeling better about Greta's state of mind, she leans back and thinks while she drives along.

"A perfect meal once, of pheasant and wild rice, cornbread and honey, with caramel custard with raspberry sauce for desert. And afterward sitting in the car watching the stars. With Mitchell, the year before we were married," she says. "Yes, I could have died that night. Gone out like a falling star." They both laugh.

They stop to change positions. Greta maneuvers over the emergency brake to the driver's seat, and Faun, who is wearing good boots, runs around the car to the passenger side. Faun won't sleep but she will rest. She would rather be driving; she trusts her own driving. She concentrates on the snow and the road, as if that will help keep them from going into the ditch. She knows she won't give up her stare-at-the-road vigil until they get to Thunder Bay, some 30 kilometers ahead. She's done this before, though this is the first time she's made the trip with Greta.

Flakes of snow, a million flakes, so white, so sparkly, like a great outdoor moving picture screen of glittering white sky. If I watch attentively, coming straight at me, straight at me, Gabriel?

The car swerves to the right. Greta grips the wheel, steering straight as the car slides along the far edge of the road, bumping against a crusty shoulder and swerving back onto the road. She stops.

"No. You're in the center of the road," Faun shouts, in a state of alarm. She hears a car, or a truck and it's quite loud. Greta looks plainly out of her mind, her eyes blank and staring straight ahead. Faun gets out and sees the lights of a snowplow some 200 yards behind them. She wastes no time getting in the driver's side, tries to push Greta over, then half sits on Greta's thigh, and with the car door open and big wet flakes of snow hitting her in the face, she pulls the car to the side of the road, or at least out of its center, and stops the car. Greta tumbles to the passenger seat, and Faun flicks on the emergency light, then leans back against the car seat with a great sigh.

The plow pulls over in front of them and the driver steps down from the cab. Faun opens the window, even though the car door is still ajar.

"Engine trouble?" he asks, peering over his fogged up glasses. He looks a bit frail for a truck driver, Faun thinks.

"No, just the damn snow," Faun tells him.

"Gets to yah, doesn't it," he says looking at them both. "Your friend okay?"

"Fine. Just a little shaken," Faun says.

"Stay behind me, you'll be all right." He leans down close. "Don't lose me, hey. No more'en thirty, forty feet behind, but don't get too close, in case I slide." He walks back to his plow without waiting for an answer, assuming

21

they'll have enough sense to follow his path and his guiding light in the now near white-out conditions.

Faun gently shakes Greta by the shoulder.

"Greta."

Greta shakes her head and sinks back into the passenger seat.

"It's okay," Faun tells her. "You get hypnotized, the snow coming down like that mile after mile."

Faun pulls out and catches up with the snowplow, lining up the front of the car with the blinking orange plow lights. They follow the slow yellow light of the plow without passing another car coming or going the entire 20 kilometers into Thunder Bay. The plow honks as it turns in at a truck stop at the north edge of town. They toot back, but continue down Center Street.

The craft store is closed, but the coffee shop next door is still open. The wind howls and a whirl of snow spins inside as they close the door of the café. A man in overalls is eating mashed potatoes and meatloaf at one of the tables and Dorothy looks up from her newspaper.

"Well, Faun Lake, of all people," she says, setting down the paper. "You're down here on a day like this?" She comes around the counter and gives Faun a friendly hug, and Faun introduces Greta.

"And this here's Ernie," she fans back her hand toward the man with the mashed potatoes, who nods back and touches his hand to the tip of an invisible hat brim.

"Now you take a table back here," she tells them, "away from the door." Faun and Greta leave their coats at the table and head for the restroom and Dorothy gives Ernie a refill of coffee. When the women return, Dorothy has steaming hot coffee waiting for them, plus real cream in a pitcher, so they won't have to use the fake packets of creamer set out on each table. Dorothy is on the phone behind the counter.

"Dorothy makes crocheted toilet-paper holders,"

Faun says. "No really, don't laugh. She's very talented. They're like old-fashioned dollies, made very tight at the bottom, and she makes either white ones, or ones that look like fruit–strawberries or purple grapes usually. You'll see some tomorrow at the shop. She used to have them in the restrooms here but someone stole one once so she doesn't keep any back there now. Tourists probably."

"I didn't mean to laugh, it just sounds funny. I wish I could crochet, but I can't do it. I can't keep the holes even. I wanted to make curtains for the bedroom windows in my cabin," Greta says.

"What'll you have?" Dorothy says coming over with an order pad. "You must be starved, coming all this way in a storm. Try the soup and pie. Chicken vegetable with dumplings. My dumplings. Ernie finished off the mashed potatoes. He sure likes his mashed potatoes," she says, glancing over at Ernie. "The pie is raspberry, made from fresh frozen. Berries from Jensen's farm."

"Sounds perfect," Faun says.

"Same for me," Greta says.

"Dorothy's pies are worth going through storms for," Faun tells Greta.

"Hah. You guys," Dorothy says, laughing as she goes off to get the soup. "You have to wait a sec for the dumplings," she tells them over her shoulder, "I make them fresh."

"I really need this normal place and a bowl of normal soup," Greta says, shaking her head. "How do you tell if you're going crazy?" she asks, not sure if she's asking seriously.

"I think you lose your sense of humor. You have nothing to worry about. It's just the snow, all that snow coming at you. You're all right," Faun says.

"I hope so," she answers, but she's scared. She saw Gabriel on the road in the snow; floating above the road in the snow.

Chapter 5

Beginnings: Gabriel is dancing in the second floor studio. From across the street Greta watches him leap across the room of many windows, his form concealed behind the brick, then revealed at the next window. He dances from window to window as if he is within the frames of a filmstrip.

The first floor door is open. She climbs the stairs half way and stops. She can hear the thumping of Gabriel's feet as he dances on the wooden floor, and the thud of each hard landing. This sound of dancing human feet always surprises her. She stands for five minutes, maybe longer, waiting for courage to go up. Should she, dare she? He may be angry. Will he remember her? Will she be interrupting?

The door to the studio is open. She leans against its frame and watches him dance, forgetting herself, seeing only the dance, his leaps above the great oak floor, his spins through the sunlight of the windows. She is aware of nothing else, just the dance, until he lands with a leap in front of her, breathless. Gabriel takes her hand and pulls her into the room. He helps her with her slippers. Her fingers tremble as he tightens her laces.

That night, when she was trying to fall asleep, she was still in a state of glory, she couldn't come down to earth. How could she tell anyone what it was like, dancing with Gabriel? It wasn't anything she could explain. She could as soon call her mother on the phone and tell her she had a lovely afternoon being a bird; that a golden eagle had invited her to fly with him over Spirit Mountain. They had soared and spun and floated and now she was trying to sleep, but she was still an inch or so above her bed, spinning when she closed her eyes and mother, no, she hadn't started drinking. Dancers never drink.

Gabriel's early years: "Exceptional musical, language, and acrobatic abilities."

"Can that be done?" Mrs. Darling asks Mrs. Door, the principal. They stand at the window of Mrs. Darling's first grade room which overlooks the play yard. Gabriel has walked the length of the top metal rail of the swings and now stands on one end of the rail, hopping rhythmically from one foot to the other. He takes a quick little jump, seemingly without looking at the pole, and slides down to the ground. They watch as he runs around the outskirts of the playing field, doing front flips in the air, effortless back flips, and he ends his romp galloping back to the other children where he slides in the dust to a quick stop in front of Suzie, who throws up her arms in delight and giggles.

"The grandfather was in the circus," Mrs. Door says. "An acrobat, I believe. Trapeze artists," though she isn't sure about that. She heard it from Mr. Quillan, who teaches sixth grade, and a lot of his comments end with "I'm pretty sure. Yes, must be so, must be so."

Mrs. Darling doesn't know what to make of Gabriel. She thinks he's like a character from a book of the type she doesn't understand. But then what can you expect, she tells herself, with parents like his. His mother picks him up early each day for "lessons" but they've never said what kind of lessons. She knows from Gabriel's file that he speaks French, Italian, Spanish and German, but she thinks his mother calls to him in Russian when she stops to pick him up. Even their car is odd, some combination of a Model T and Jaguar, and black, like the mother's clothes. She always wears a peculiar hat with a broad front brim and she laughs, even when it's below zero. Mrs. Darling infers from the car that the family may be involved in some type of general gangsterism. The father has a connection to music, but she doesn't know just what he does. Mrs. Darling thinks Gabriel's "lessons" may be: (1) Russian lessons; (2) circus lessons, such as juggling; (3) lessons of an usual scientific nature; or (4) violin lessons, and she hopes it's the latter.

Gabriel is far beyond his age group in his school work, even though he is out for weeks at a time. They no longer move students ahead grades like they used to, and when Gabriel returns from a trip to New York or London or Paris, he brings a postcard for each child in the class, and asks Mrs. Door for permission to talk to the class about his travels. His fellow students genuinely like him. He's always fun and never acts like he's showing off. He spouts facts and figures, interesting anecdotes, and answers the children's questions as though he is a humanities professor, as well as a fellow seven-year-old student.

Chapter 6

Greta has an appointment with a psychologist for 3:30 this afternoon and she's making her list. Dr. Winkle said she should bring a list of her favorite childhood horrors, and suggests she have at least three. Her confidence in Dr. Winkle is starting off poorly, but she has no choice as he is the only psychologist in this part of town. She found his name in a free paper at the arts cooperative. She makes a list: (1) coal man; (2) nuns; (3) leeches. She adds: (4) liver; (5) her brother chasing her with slimy garbage from the sink drain after the dishes were washed; (6) night crawlers on sidewalks after a rain; and (7) dresses with puffy sleeves. So what has any of this to do with seeing Gabriel in the snow, she wonders?

Dr. Winkle's office is in a corner brick building, on the second floor next to a dentist's office. She can hear the low buzzing of the dentist's drill as she lies down on the couch. Dr. Winkle's long nose seems to be pointing at Greta and she associates it with the dental drill. He smells like old cigar butts and chewing gum, and his small eyes are hooded like a lizard, but he has a gentleness when he smiles that helps her relax. She tries to ignore his badly bitten nails.

"No, Gabriel was never my lover," she tells him, "though we were lovers when we danced." He cannot understand this. "Our spirits made love," she tells him, "while we danced." Dr. Winkle nods his head, and says "I see, I see," but she sees that he doesn't. Dr. Winkle wants to know if Gabriel and the coal man looked alike. Greta, normally a very patient person, has already decided to finish her hour, pay the doctor, and never come back. It was a mistake to come. But she tells him she doesn't really know what the coal man looked like, he was always covered with coal dust so she couldn't tell. Gabriel is made of air, light, and now, snow. The coal man would come to the back door and holler out "coal man" in a loud and serious voice. Then he would open the outer door of the coal chute to the coal bin, tilt the truck dumpster, affix the slide, and down would come the coal, a black avalanche of coal crashing and banging its way into the empty coal bin; a wonderful and thrilling terror to Greta and her brother. There was always something exotic and secret about the coal.

They take a break and Greta gets up to stretch. She looks out the window while Dr. Winkle heats water for tea in a lop-sided metal container with a door, which whistles like a train when the water is hot. Outside, it's still snowing, but not so heavily as yesterday. He sets both cups of raspberry leaf tea on a table by the couch and tells Greta he'll be back in a moment. He disappears through an inner office door at the side of his office, seemingly toward the dentist's office. Greta can see the shadows of two men, and hear their conferring voices through the opaque greenish glass window of the dividing door.

The tea is delicious. She is nearly finished when Dr. Winkle returns. He settles back with his tea and tells Greta she is afraid of men. She associates men with the coal man and she is afraid of falling down the coal chute to hell, so can only make love when she is dancing, which is not love, but an illusion. He also tells her that he would like a stained-glass hanging for his office window, and he'll look at her glass work at the craft store before they close today.

She can tell Dr. Winkle is in a good mood now, feeling it is no longer necessary for him to listen, he can just talk, which he prefers. He tells Greta to relax, asks if she wants more tea, which she doesn't. She settles back comfortably on the couch, and Dr. Winkle begins the story of his Aunt Ruth, his grandmother's sister, from whose garden has come the raspberry leaves for their tea.

"Ruth lives about ten kilometers north of town on Wall Street. Oh, it's just a dirt road, but we call it Wall Street because she owns the property up and down both sides of the road–good farm land. She's filthy rich. But you wouldn't know it to look at her. She wears dresses made of flour sacks. Makes them herself on an old treadle sewing machine. Filthy rich." He nods at Greta and smiles. His teeth are tiny, but very white. He goes on to tell about Ruth's penny-pinching background, how she had to pay her brothers for a ride to town when she was a teenager. The family made their money in real estate, buying up farms when prices were low and times were hard for many, but they held onto the land, and rented out the acreage they couldn't work themselves.

Greta finds no connection between his Aunt Ruth and herself, since there is none, but still she listens—her hour will be up in ten minutes. She doesn't want to talk more to this peculiar man. She'll keep Gabriel to herself and get sleeping pills, even if Faun says they're addicting and you don't have proper dreams when you take them.

"Ruth is in her late 70's, and the only one left," he says, snapping one finger nail nub against another.

After Dr. Winkle has walked Greta through Ruth's garden, row by row, past the peas and beans, and cabbages, and straight into the strawberry patch with the biggest, sweetest berries in Canada, the session comes to an end. Greta puts on her coat and gets out her checkbook to pay Dr. Winkle, but he says "No, no cost. No charge today." She doesn't like this at all.

"I'll just write one," she says, and writes a check for $75.00, since she has no idea what an hour with a "real" psychologist would cost, but she wants to be fair and she wants to get out. He refuses to take the check, so she leaves it on the table by the teacups. At the door, Dr. Winkle tells her to get some coal, put it in a little basket, and look at it, think about it–talk to it if she likes, and next time they'll talk about the coal, and about her father. He gives her a new red toothbrush as she leaves.

Chapter 7

Gabriel Dimetri Perez
– from the reviews:
"ballet will never be the same"
"there are times one looks for tricks, in order to explain"
"a delicate, distant kind of airiness"
"an original quality of awareness all his own"
"Gabriel, the archangel"
"Saturday night, an audience was transported to paradise"
"unaware of an audience"
"the dancer's dancer"
"women swooned in the aisles"
"dances as if before gods"
"the greatest dancer since Nijinsky"
"I gave up on the review"
"Gabriel withdraws from the ballet scene"
"impulsive decision"
"unfounded rumors of failing health"
"final performance"

At present Gabriel's studio is one large rectangular room with hardwood floors, high arched windows set in brick walls, one partially-mirrored wall, and an end wall featuring a large round abstract stained-glass window of deep blue and purple, forest green, velvety red and pure winter white. A gold oriental screen with white cranes sits in a corner next to a grand piano. An alcove leads to a bathroom, and next to it is a small refrigerator-less kitchen, with a wood-burning stove, microwave, and a calendar of doors from around the world. A postcard of blue ice from Glen Gould is tacked to the wall.

The studio has no furniture. No bed. No chairs. And no phone. One Chagall. The music library is in a second alcove behind the piano. Gabriel looks among the "S's" of the CDs for Erwin Schulhoff, chooses his Quartet No. 1, to match the intensity of his mood. He selects his music intuitively and thinks of his music collection as his tarot cards, and his friends. Every day now he dances. Before, he could do only exercises. He could teach his students, demonstrate a few measures, but could dance, really dance, maybe once a month. Yet everyday to condition himself, he would dance within. He would sit in meditation in the center of his studio listening to the music. He could dance in his mind, and it gave him great joy, as well as a sorrow he could not put to words, and which he knew would bring on the pain.

Today he has his freedom back, and he dances all four movements, then bows down on one knee in silent tribute to Schulhoff, and coming out of the rapture of the dance and back into his own body, he begins to weep. He walks about the studio, brushing away salty, stinging tears, so thankful for the music, for the return of his body, and thankful to the ancient Chinese who were crazy enough to dream up acupuncture.

Gabriel gathers up the little notes people are always slipping under his door because he has no phone in the studio. He has no tolerance for the ringing of phones, or the hum of a refrigerator. The sound of any motor annoys him, with the exception of the motor of a boat.

"I don't think I should have to dance to Stravinsky— his music makes me *too* nervous. Please leave me a note after class. Don't talk to me about this!" – Joy

"I really need a private lesson." – Jennifer

"Donna can't come to class tomorrow. She has bronchitis. When are you going to get e-mail?" – Donna's mother.

There is also an invitation to a party at the Bizetti's

for Friday night. Why didn't they mail it? Because he has no phone do they think he refuses to use the postal service?

And from his fishing pal:

"Come for duck dinner tonight at 6:00. – Dave

Dave drops the duck bones, one by one, onto the center of the plastic blue checkered tablecloth and leans forward as far as his big belly will allow. He studies the bones.

"I see changes," he says. "Coming for to carry me – h-o-m-e," he sings in a deep whispery voice.

Dave and Gabriel are both now concentrating on the bones.

"The duck is trying to tell us something," Dave says, narrowing his eyes as he leans in close to the meatless bones. He places both hands flat on the table as if to hold it down while he holds his breath. His hiccup breaks the spell. Dave pours himself the last of the Beaujolais, sniffs it, and swivels it around in his glass. Gabriel pours himself another mineral water, squeezes in lemon juice, along with a few seeds, and they clink glasses in a toast to the duck.

"To the duck. May his life not have been in vain," Gabriel says.

"Damn cold, that day we shot him," Dave says.

"I didn't shoot him," Gabriel says.

"That's right. You were shooting stars."

Gabriel feels his face aflame, embarrassed all these months later, remembering how he shot at the first ducks they saw, even though they were a mile away. He didn't have a chance of hitting one, but he didn't know that. No one taught him how to hunt, or how to fish. Dave just looked at him, and later made a comment to a buddy about his long-range shooting, which of course had just scared off the ducks.

They had gone down the lake that morning in the dark with the stars still thick in the sky, dropping anchor at the edge of a thicket of reeds. The water was icy as they eased the dozen or so black wood decoys onto the lake, then sat waiting in the cold for dawn, listening to the oars creak in their sockets as the boat rocked gently up and down.

Gabriel was horrified when they pulled in the ducks Dave had shot. Two of the ducks were still alive and fluttering broken wings, and one tried to swim away, its head crooked, demented with pain. He had wanted to shoot Dave then and there, wring his neck and toss him into the icy waters of White Deer Lake.

Dave pushes his plate aside and leans back in his chair, picks up his tattered paperback copy of *The Upanishads*, and reads:

"The sage must distinguish between knowledge and wisdom. Knowledge is of things, acts and relations. To become one with him is the only wisdom." – V. Mundaka.

"To become one with the duck," Dave says.

"To become one with our enemies," Gabriel says.

"To our enemies' enemies," Dave says, finishing his wine.

Again they contemplate the bones.

"To fly without wings, that's what the bones are saying," Gabriel says with finality. Gabriel plays with the wishbone, running its greasy edge along his own clavicle, considering how a man might distinguish between knowledge and wisdom. How can an animal enjoy its animal self? And why was the mallard so delicious?

"Come on, I want to show you something. Up on the roof," Dave says, looking at his watch. It's a few minutes before 1:00 am. Dave puts on his coat, ready to go. Gabriel sits at the table with his hands folded in front of him while Dave waits patiently beside a tattered black and white poster of Bob Dylan in the stairwell.

"Okay," Gabriel says, getting up abruptly. He slips on his sheepherder's jacket and follows Dave up the stairs. Dave opens a window at the landing and climbs out to the flat roof of the veranda. Joining him, Gabriel steps out next to a bowl of snow. Several bowls of snow are scattered about the flat roof top, some on foot-high logs set on end, though most of the logs are topped with wooden cigar boxes filled with tall rectangles of snow. Next to the railing a couple of ski poles are sticking out at odd angles. Big Dave sweeps the snow from the bowls and boxes with a tiny whisk broom to uncover frozen birdseed. His quick movements are precise; he's careful not to brush away the seed, the treasure of his snowy architectural dig.

"You need some umbrellas up here. Something," Gabriel tells him. "What do you do when we get several feet?"

"It's not that deep. This side doesn't get hit too bad. Over here though," Dave says, stepping over the bowls to the ski poles. This is the new thing. They're lined up with the satellite." He stands looking at Gabriel, calculating the difference in their height, surprised at how close they are. Dave had thought he was much taller than Gabriel. He brushes the snow off an up-ended log and sits down, explaining how you look at the top of the left ski pole, and use it as a sight line to the right ski pole—that it will line up with the Northern Star, just off the lower right star of the bowl of the big dipper, marking the path of a satellite.

"It should be here in just a minute," he says, and gets up so Gabriel can have the astronomer's seat. Gabriel sits on the cold log and matches the ski pole to the marker star and waits. The stars are thick and bright in the dark Canadian sky and the satellite is easy to spot well before it reaches the marker star. Dave pulls a notebook out of his inner jacket pocket and, with considerable satisfaction and self importance, enters the time in his log book. Gabriel is appropriately impressed with the accuracy of Dave's "high tech" ski pole astronomy equipment, and with his creativity. They watch the satellite cross the sky until it's out of sight, then look for constellations. Dave quizzes Gabriel on some of the major ones he's pointed out to him before, and they are both pleased when Gabriel finds the three stars of Orion's belt–Orion, the Mighty Hunter, and the Bear. They climb back in through the window, well satisfied with themselves and the sky.

Driving home, Gabriel thinks of how personally he takes the Canadian sky, especially at night. He almost thinks of it as a friend, and is sure Dave does too. He enjoys Dave. He is one of the few people who has no interest in dance, or in Gabriel's past, and so he can enjoy this ordinary side of himself when they are together. Dave is a car mechanic with an unusual assortment of interests, and a full-service garage just outside Winnipeg. They ended up friends when Tia, Dave's ex-wife, slid into Gabriel's car in a snow storm and they all spent the night at Dave's. She wasn't quite his ex-wife then, but close to it, going by the loud argument he overheard in the early morning before he got up. Tia manages a health food store near Winnipeg, makes her own carrot juice, grows her own organic vegetables, part of which she sells in the store. Gabriel has been a regular customer for two years now, though he's never told Dave. Tia doesn't eat meat. She couldn't even stand the idea, let alone the smell. When Dave would fry a batch of trout, or venison hamburgers she'd take off, and then open all the windows when she got back, even in winter. It was a doomed marriage. Simply a matter of dietary differences.

Dave and Gabriel get together probably once a month, sometimes to watch a hockey game, or just to eat and drink. Or they go fishing. Gabriel was flattered when Dave came to him for a sympathetic ear, just after his divorce–it was such a novelty for Gabriel. Men rarely thought of him as someone they could talk to. People tended to set him above themselves. But not Dave, who thought of Gabriel as a slightly retarded brother, due to his inexperience in the woods. That first night he came to the house Dave was so drunk it was a wonder he arrived at all. Gabriel kept getting up, following him around, ready to catch him if he fell. He sniffled and stumbled around the kitchen, telling Gabriel how sad he was when he looked out the kitchen window at his lonely compost heap and how bare and forlorn the spot on the counter was where she used to keep her juicer. He moaned over his poor lonely bed, the poor lonely chair, everything lonely and bare and empty. His repetition made Gabriel think of a children's story, then suddenly Dave wanted to go home, though he could barely stand up. He said he would hurry right back, that he needed to get his Dylan collection. He just had to play "the string bean song" for Gabriel. Gabriel suggested that Dave sit down on the couch in the living room for a minute first, which he did, and immediately slumped over and fell asleep.

Dave had pretty much adjusted to living by himself after about a year, and he and Gabriel were quite good friends by then. Gabriel looked forward to seeing Dave, who was a very accepting person, as was Tia, but everyone had their limits, apparently. She still cared about him and would ask Gabriel how Dave was doing over a bunch of beets, or whatever he was buying at the health food store. Gabriel shopped for groceries intuitively, as he choose music, according to what his body craved, or was it his spirit? Could a spirit crave beets? Spinach? Oat bran? As most dancers, he had always been careful about his physical self, and although he occasionally ate meat, it was never more than a few times a year and he would feel renewed afterward, such as tonight after the duck dinner. But he knew tomorrow he would feel heavy and leaden and wouldn't be able to dance.

Dave had brought him out of the dance studio and out into nature. He took him down the lake to see eagles taking off from their nests. They watched with binoculars as the birds rose into the sky, their powerful wings flapping slowly, surprisingly slowly, to rise upward. They took their time. He learned from them.

Now Gabriel has his own motor boat, an old wooden row boat, and a red canoe. He takes long trips down White Deer Lake by himself, docks his boat at a lodge ten miles down the lake where he stores his canoe, then canoes along the lake edge about a half mile to his favorite lake, which is actually a bay, Apollo Bay, which Dave tells him is officially Turtle Bay. The left side of the bay is covered with white water lilies where he's seen moose wading and nibbling their lunch. He has his own rock, where he eats his lunch. It's next to a sand beach where he can easily pull in the canoe, and the rock slopes down to the lake and points to a tiny island where blueberries grow. On his rock he can sleep in the sun, watch the turtles sunning on logs and boulders in the bay, or watch geese and ducks and other birds come and go. Sometimes he swims, trying not to think about the snapping turtles. There is rarely anyone on this part of the lake, and only once has he encountered anyone in the bay, and then just a couple of fisherman, who soon left because of the turtles. No one likes the nasty experience of hooking a turtle, Dave told him.

Gabriel is almost home. The drive from Dave's always goes by fast. When he pulls into the driveway, he sees Jennifer's Volkswagen bug sitting by his garage.

She's done this before, but not in such cold weather, and it scares him. What if she's fallen asleep with the motor on? He's relieved to see her get out of the car and wave at him. He drives into the garage slowly, hoping he can send her on her way without a scene. It's 2:10 am and he's dead tired–the sleepless nights after the acupuncture must be catching up with him. Jennifer is a clumsy dancer, too big really, but she works hard and loves ballet with a genuine passion, so Gabriel enjoys working with her as a student, if only she would leave it at that. He dreads these encounters and tries hard to remain aloof and professorial on the one hand, while on the other, knowing it's an absolute necessity to be warm and encouraging with his young students. The sheer physicality of ballet brings emotions to the surface and he knows it's important to be careful, to be thoughtful of their youthful sensitivities. Before he taught, he could handle the advances of women; it was either yes or no, they were on equal footing. He knows he is a good teacher and brings out the best in each student, if they would just stop falling for him.

"Mr. Perez," I thought you might be lonely. It's such a cold night. Don't look at me like that. Am I so bad? I'm too ugly, you don't like me," Jennifer says, covering her face with her mittened hands, already starting to cry before Gabriel has said a word.

"No, please don't call my mother. I know you're going to call my mother."

"Jennifer, come inside. It's cold. Now there's no reason to cry," he says. She's so lovely under the porch light bundled up in a big down parka, her complexion so baby soft. Gabriel would love to carry her inside and up to his bed, lose himself in her soft sweetness. But they go inside and Gabriel calls her mother, who tells him to keep her there. "Don't let her drive. We'll be right out. Be there in ten minutes," Jennifer's mother says. "Her Dad will drive the bug and Jennifer will ride in the pick-up with me."

"Well, they're on their way," he says, hanging up the phone. "Tea?" Gabriel heats water for tea, while Jennifer sits at the table dabbing at her eyes and nose with a tissue.

"I'm flattered Jennifer," he says. "But first of all, I'm your teacher, and second, I'm too old for you. You should be dating someone in your class. What are you this year, aren't you a sophomore?"

"Junior," she says. She's stopped crying now but is quite sullen.

"And, most important, I care about you, and that's why I called your folks," he says. They sip chamomile tea and wait for her parents. Gabriel asks about her classes, her interests aside from ballet.

"I'm interested in you," she says matter-of-factly.

"Besides that. What else do you like?"

"Well, they're doing this play at school, *Ten Little Indians*. Officially they call it *And Then There Were None*, because that's more correct, you know, but it's a murder mystery. I haven't told anyone yet," she leans toward him confidentially, "but I was thinking of trying out."

Gabriel nods, watching her shy enthusiasm, thinking she could well use something like that–a second artistic outlet for her passionate nature.

"My speech teacher last year said I have the voice for it. She says I project very well."

"Yes, you have a strong voice. Do it Jenny. I think it's a great idea. When are auditions?"

"Tomorrow, after school."

"Heavens, and here you are up this late. Here they are," he says, hearing the pick-up come down the drive.

"Oh Lord. The last time I came out here, in September, when it rained? She took the bug away for a month."

"What will she do? What do you think she'll do?" he asks.

"My dad won't say anything, and my mom will glare. She glares so hard it looks like her face'll crack off like in *The Mummy*. You know that movie? That's one of my favorites. I love when Boris Karloff chants in ancient Egyptian. Oh!" she says, now quite happy and awake.

"Mostly they just yell at each other. Blame each other for me being bad. They'll say things like *What kind of example are you? And where were you in September? And, okay Queen Elizabeth, since you know it all, you handle it*." She's laughing now.

Gabriel opens the door and quietly tells her parents she just wanted to talk about school, that they really shouldn't be too hard on her.

He clicks off the porch light after they drive out of sight, and soon he is in bed. Ten seconds after his head hits the pillow he's sound asleep.

Chapter 8

Faun and Greta are spending a second night in Thunder Bay. The weather report is for blizzard conditions all day, with increasing snow to the north and expected to taper off during the night. They both spent the afternoon at the craft shop, except for Greta's hour down the street at Dr. Winkle's. Tonight they are at Dorothy's again; she closed the café early because of the storm and dropped off a mason jar of hot stew for Ernie at his apartment above Joe's Corner Drug.

Dorothy clicks off the TV after the late weather report. Her husband, Ron, who teaches driver's training and directs the chorus at the high school, has gone to bed early with a sore throat, and the women are lounging around the TV. Greta and Faun are in borrowed robes and the lace on Greta's robe is scratching her neck. The lace makes it seem that the robe hasn't been worn before but otherwise it's soft and cozy.

"Hot chocolate?" Dorothy asks. They all want some.

"With or without Amaretto?"

With, it's unanimous.

Dorothy arrives with a tray of mugs of hot chocolate, plus a bottle of Amaretto, and a scissors.

"I'll cut off that lace. I should have done it when I got it, two years ago," Dorothy says. Greta slips off the robe and Dorothy clips off the lace. "Sometimes I save things for a special occasion, like a trip to Mars. I'll crochet a pink cotton border, something with nice soft cotton," she says, handing back the robe.

Soon they've finished the hot chocolate and are sipping straight Amaretto from their mugs. Greta has passed along Aunt Ruth's gardening tips: spread wood ashes around the cabbages to keep away the slugs, be sure to dry raspberry leaves thoroughly before using for tea or you might be poisoned. And, Ruth's medicinal advice: Never eat those little silver things used to decorate cakes–they cause diabetes, cancer, and epilepsy.

"Good grief, she even knows what causes cancer," Faun laughs, stretching her legs out on the coffee table. Greta enjoys telling Faun and Dorothy about her session with Dr. Winkle. She's told them she went to him because she's been having terrible nightmares. She hasn't mentioned Gabriel. Dorothy says she was probably the only patient Dr. Winkle has seen in months, she knows him from her trips to his brother, Dr. Ted Winkle, the dentist. The shrink, Dr. Winkle comes through the inner office door and acts like he's the dental assistant, Dorothy tells them. He hands Dr. Ted Winkle dental tools occasionally, but mostly he just comes to watch. And Dr. Ted is always saying things like "Back Willie. Not so close Willie."

Faun and Greta both say "Willie Winkle" at the same time, and start laughing, while trying to be quiet since Ron is sleeping in the next room.

"And to think he's my first customer in Thunder Bay. He practically followed me back to the co-op, and bought the swan lake piece from the front window," Greta says.

"And also returned your check," Faun says. "That's probably how he gets away with it. He doesn't accept money, so no one is likely to complain."

"He did have a certificate on the wall," Greta says, thinking of how nice the colored-glass swan lake hanging looked in the craft store window in the bright snow light, and she wonders where Dr. Winkle will hang it in his office. Probably in the back window.

"I suppose you could say he has an unusual technique. Who knows, maybe he's a genius," Greta says.

"Not too likely," Dorothy says on her way into the kitchen with the tray of mugs balanced on one hand.

"And how could anyone be sure about the guy? I mean people who go to him are the ones with the problems," Greta says. "What kind of discrimination are they going to have? They're probably not very sure of their own opinions or they wouldn't be seeing him."

"Well let's all say goodnight to Wee Willie Winkie. I've got deliveries coming in at 6:30 in the morning–the milk truck never came today, and I've got eggs coming in too. Plus I have pies to bake." Dorothy knows she can count on Ernie to be there early shoveling her out so she'll open for breakfast.

It's 11:00 o'clock when they pull out the hide-a-bed and roll-away. Greta and Faun plan to leave early in the morning too. The sky has cleared so the roads should be plowed and sanded by morning. Greta is going to send Dorothy the dimensions of her bedroom window so she can crochet curtains for her, in exchange for a stained-glass piece featuring fruit. Greta falls asleep with images of grapes and oranges and coal, almost sure that she'll sleep through the night with peaceful dreams.

———

The pale early morning sun is marked by the cold weather halo of the sun dog, and the land is beautiful under a fresh blanket of snow. Drifts well up against hills and barns, and haystacks and fence posts are topped with tall white mounds of snow. Greta's roof has a poor slant; she'll have to get out the ladder and scrape snow with the old pole after digging though the inevitable drift she'll face at her front door. She hopes Karloff can get out this morning and plow her driveway. He'll do Faun's too, if he can get out, but her place is never as bad as Greta's. Faun's house is surrounded by thick firs, and has little cleared space, which is fine in winter, but in summer it's thick with mosquitoes.

Greta wiggles her toes, pleased with her new boots, which are fleece-lined and come up to her knees. She had them conditioned with mink oil right at the store. Her old boots would have lasted another couple of years if a mouse family hadn't moved into her left boot in late summer. She won't leave these out in the shed. Faun reminded her that your boots can save your life up here. Your boots are your life, she said. While she was trying on boots in Thunder Bay, Greta kept picturing Millie's four-toed foot in the sauna, so she choose the warmest and most practical pair, not the most expensive, but nearly so.

Millie lost her toe to frostbite as a child, walking home from school on a bitter cold day. She was wearing boots, but with thin cotton socks that offered little protection against a surprise October snow storm. Luckily, she had brought her new angora birthday muff for Show and Tell, otherwise she would likely have lost fingers as well as the toe. Millie always tells how Allen, a boy in her class, brought his father's glass eye for Show and Tell that day, somehow making it seem the two calamities were connected–the loss of the toe, and the missing eye. Millie hadn't liked the way some of her schoolmates wanted to touch the eye; she worried about Allen's father. What if they broke it? No one asked what he was doing that day with his eye at school, and it troubled her. In fact that's what she kept thinking about when she was in the hospital. Millie had told the story recently in the sauna, though they had all heard the story a number of times before. She always talked about it as though it happened just a month or so ago, rather than 60 years past. Tillie is the one who tells them–rather guiltily it seems to Greta, that she had been home with a bad cold that day.

Faun has said little since they left Thunder Bay. She is a good listener, a serious person. Greta admires her Garbo-esque profile, and her short silky gray hair which she sets off with richly colored hand-woven shawls and sweaters. She wears the same silver arrow earrings most every day.

Faun grew up in Toronto, studied theater design, and married Mitchell Lake, a cardiologist who died of a heart attack in his early 40s. She then took up knitting, joined a sewing club with her daughter, Monique, who died in a horrendous car/train wreck seven years ago, after which Faun moved to Red Otter, bought a house on the lake, and a loom.

Faun turns off the radio and asks Greta to find a tape in the glove compartment.

Ghost Stories by Robertson Davies, *The Plow that Broke the Plains*, or *National Anthems of the World*? Or wait, this one, "film music by Nina Roto, side one; French film music, side two," she reads from the label.

"French film music," Faun says. "Okay with you?"

"Sure," she says, sliding it into the tape player.

By the time they reach Red Otter they have listened to all of the tapes, including the ghost stories, and are on a second hearing of the film music from France when they stop at Don's Grocery, pulling in just before the store closes for the day. They buy the bare necessities–bread, milk and fruit, plus ice cream.

Jeanne Moreau is singing "Le Tourbillon" from *Jules and Jim* when they make the turn-off to the lake. They've received more snow than Thunder Bay and it's piled all the way up to the blue letters on Faun's mail box: Rte. 9, F. Lake. Faun steps out and scoops out the mail, which she tosses into the back seat. They're both relieved to see Faun's drive has been plowed, which means Karloff has been around and Greta's drive will have been plowed too. Faun drives past the Hanson's, the only cabin between her place and Greta's. They can hear Tom Hanson out chopping wood. Greta's cabin is the last one on the road before the woods. Halfway down Greta's driveway, Faun stops the car.

"What is it?" Greta asks.

"I don't know. I have a funny feeling," Faun says.

"Well, just drive up slowly," Greta says, puzzled by Faun's apprehension, which she now feels a touch of in herself. They drive the rest of the way at 10 km/h. The driveway has been cleanly plowed and the snow shoveled away from the front door.

"Looks normal," Greta says.

"It does. But let me come in with you. Let's just see."

The porch door opens stiffly in the cold. A small drift of snow has blown in onto the porch floor, as it usually does after a storm. Greta decides she'll sweep it up later, after she unpacks and warms up the house. They both see it at the same time, and freeze: a large footprint in the light dusting of snow on the porch floor, near the inner door.

"Just Karloff, probably. Maybe he came in to check the water pipes, though mine never seem to freeze. He knows that," Greta says, trying to explain the footprint.

"Shh," Faun says. "Just listen."

They listen to the pines creaking in the wind, and in the distance, Tom chopping wood.

"Okay, let's go in," Faun says.

Greta slides her key in the lock and knows immediately that the door is unlocked, but decides not to tell Faun. She opens the door slowly, and steps inside. It looks normal, but something feels funny to her too. She puts her suitcase on the couch and is ready to check the rooms, trying to act as though she's not afraid. Yet she waits for Faun to walk from room to room with her. The bathroom door is closed nearly all the way. She's quite sure she left it wide open. To boost her confidence, she swings the door open wide and walks in. No one. Nothing. She turns on the hot water faucet to warm the pipes. There are long black hairs in the sink. She shudders, and beckons for Faun to come look.

"Oh God, Greta, we've got to get out of here. I'll call Sheriff Banzoff from my place. Come on."

They grab their purses and leave the cabin quickly. Greta doesn't lock the door, but once inside Faun's car they lock all the doors and Faun drives down the driveway as quickly as possible, considering the snowy ruts. Greta looks out the back window as they drive away. She sees no one around the cabin.

They drive in silence to Faun's house, and arrive tired but relieved to find the house looking normal. After Faun calls the sheriff, they settle themselves at the kitchen table.

"Eat something Greta. We haven't eaten since Dorothy's French toast this morning," Faun says, twirling the angel hair pasta into a manageable bite.

"An apple," Greta says. "One of those yellow ones."

Faun passes the wooden bowl of fruit to Greta, who takes an apple, and some purple grapes.

"I love grapes," Faun says, breaking off a large bunch.

"Me too," Greta says. She's hungry and the fruit tastes delicious. She can't eat the pasta. She keeps thinking of the brochure Karloff got from the vet with a color picture of long stringy heart worms. Bandit died of heart worm, and now Greta expects the pasta on her plate to start squirming. She knows she'd never sleep if she ate any of it, at least tonight.

Faun clears the table, and comes back with a fresh pot of coffee. Her coffee is always delicious and clear because she grinds the beans and puts an egg shell in with the grounds.

"Caffeine free," she says, filling two gold-edged porcelain cups. They drink their coffee and wait for the sheriff to return from Greta's.

"I don't like this waiting. It makes me think of Monique, and the time of the accident," Faun says. "But I don't feel sad. I mean, I feel close to Monique at times, as though she's with me, part of me. I hate to admit it, but I think I feel closer to her with her gone, now, than when she was alive. Isn't life just, oh, inexplicable?" she shakes her head, and rubs the side of her cup, as if to invoke a genie, or Monique.

"You said it," Greta says, wondering why she's had no sense of Gabriel's presence for the last three days, and realizes she misses him and she knows what Faun is talking about, that sense of closeness. But how can she miss him? Really now, how?

They're both tired by the time Sheriff Banzoff pulls up. His report doesn't alarm them–they had both been imagining the worst, probably after the ghost stories in the car during the drive north.

The place is basically clean, he tells them. He found more black hairs–long ones, on the quilt in the bedroom. And an empty can of beans under the sink that he didn't think could have been there for more than a day, but no dirty pans or dishes.

"Who ever it was, was very careful and cleaned up after himself," he says. And he talked to Karloff, who hadn't noticed anything unusual this morning when he plowed the drive, though he said the shed door was half open when he went to get the shovel, but he hadn't thought anything of it at the time.

"Are you sure you locked up when you went down to Thunder Bay?" he asks Greta.

It was quite early, and she hadn't been sleeping well, that's true, but she thinks she must have locked the door, though she never locks it when she makes a quick trip into Red Otter.

"I probably locked it," Greta says.

"Well, I found some snowshoe tracks, just a couple, down next to the boat house. The storm covered everything else. It could've been a trapper caught out in the blizzard. You know there are some Cree families out there, way back in the woods past the falls. They might have trap lines up this way. Doesn't Latos buy maple syrup from one of those guys? I'm pretty sure they come in, maybe twice a year. I'll talk to him in the morning. I think you can go on home, Greta. I don't think we have anything to worry about here."

"Or stay here tonight and go home in the morning," Faun suggests.

"I'd like to do that," she tells Faun, as she yawns. It's going to be okay, she decides.

They thank Sheriff Banzoff and Faun offers him a cup of coffee, but he says it's too late, and wishes them a good evening and tells them to lock up, just to be on the safe side, and he'll come out or call in the morning, after he talks to Latos.

After the sheriff leaves, their tension pretty much dissipates, and both Faun and Greta start yawning excessively.

"Good night, good night, good night," Fauns says finally.

"Night," Greta says through a last yawn.

Oddly enough, after the excitement of the day, both Faun and Greta are relaxed and thinking of little else other than sleep. In Faun's guest room, Greta is cozy and comfortable under a mountainous cloud of a feather bed, where she quickly falls asleep.

The White Place - Rest here in this emptiness, in this place of nothing–in this snow.

Chapter 9

Gabriel is hoping Dave will like the present he bought for him: *The Canadian Sky–Four Seasons*. He's wrapped it in paper he found with suns and moons, which isn't Christmas paper, but nevertheless seems right. He has time for only a quick stop to drop it off before he leaves for rehearsal. He's doing *The Nutcracker* this Christmas, for the first time in six years.

Getting out of the car, he sees Dave has decorated an outdoor tree for the birds. The spruce by the back door is covered with scraps of food tied on with grocery twine, whole pieces of bread are tied around various branch tips, like pine needle hotdogs, and various unidentifiable items deck the boughs. A small strand of popcorn dangles from the top of the tree, and a rope of cranberries circles the lower branches. The main feeder beside the spruce is piled high with birdseed and Dave has attached a wire cage filled with suet next to his front door. Gabriel is sure Dave is the only person in Canada who has suet nailed to his house, rather than to a tree or post.

Dave has the door open and is waiting for Gabriel, a chunk of blue cheese in his hand, which apparently he has been eating like a candy bar.

"Like my tree? Come on in. I've got chickadees, blue jays, buntings, sparrows. Wait'll you see what I got. I got a present from Tia." He rushes into the living room to find the present.

"She gave me a camera," he says, hurrying back. "And here, see her note," he hands it to Gabriel before taking the last bite of the blue cheese.

Dear Dave,

I hope you enjoy the camera. Shoot some photos instead of guns! –Tia.

"That's very nice," Gabriel says, handing back the note.

"Zoom lens," Dave says. "I thought I'd start on the chickadees."

Gabriel gives Dave the sky book. He opens it immediately, and starts to read. When he turns the page Gabriel has to remind him he can't stay long, he has to drive into Winnipeg, but he's pleased Dave is already absorbed in the book.

"You get a book too," Dave says, handing Gabriel his Christmas present, wrapped in creased and wrinkled paper with a birthday cake and balloon motif. Gabriel's book is called *Wild Life of North America,* with a wolf on the cover and a turtle on the back. Dave skims the book, which has a lot of photographs–more wolves and turtles– also deer, moose, eagles, bear, chipmunks, fish and birds. There is a long chapter on birds: "More than 150 varieties of waterfowl migrate to the southern edges of Lake Manitoba each year," he reads.

He slaps Dave on the back. "Damn," he says, "Thanks. Gotta run."

Back in his car, he says, "I talk like Dave," and laughs. He's happy. It's a good Christmas.

———

A week after their return from Thunder Bay, Greta is at the top of the ladder, knocking snow off the roof with a bamboo fishing pole when Faun drives up. Light snow is floating down in small clumps.

"Easy snow," she says, climbing down to Faun. "Not that crusty stuff we had last week."

"50.7 inches. That's our average snowfall," Faun says as they take off their boots on the porch. "I heard it on the radio this morning. Churchill gets 77 inches. Beautiful moccasins. A Christmas gift?"

Greta tells how she found the soft deerskin moccasins wrapped in a rabbit skin tied up with rawhide on her front steps yesterday morning when she went out to the bird feeder, and that they're a perfect fit. Indeed, she's never had such comfortable shoes. They both admire the craftsmanship of the soft gold moccasins. Greta slips them on and walks in silent comfort into the kitchen, while Faun follows in her plain stockinged feet.

While the tea steeps, Greta opens her present. A woven skirt in shades of blue, with a fringed hemline. Faun gets a stained-glass window which Greta says is for her outhouse.

"You can enjoy it when the pipes freeze," Greta tells her. Several of the cabins have an outhouse for such emergency use.

"Oh, but it's so beautiful, you really don't want me to put in out there, do you?" Faun laughs.

"Of course. It'll look great against the old weathered wood, don't you think?" They are both anxious to see how it will look. Greta reaches behind her and grabs a letter from the counter. She holds it out so Faun can see who it's from.

"The Thunder Bay shrink?"

"That's right. Dr. Winkle. He wants to visit me. Says he has business in Red Otter. Of course no one ever has business in Red Otter, especially in winter. He got my address from the craft shop. Says while he's here he wants to commission another stained-glass piece.

"Could you do a snow scene with some rabbits?" she reads. "I would like it if they were quite cheerful. And could you put in a few pine trees. Seven would be nice. How is the toothbrush holding up?"

Greta shakes her head as she pours tea.

"What will you do?" Faun asks.

"I don't know. Any ideas?"

They ponder the situation in silence as they sip their tea.

"Can I see the moccasins again?" Faun asks.

Greta slips off both slippers and they each fondle one of the baby soft moccasins, and end up laughing at the same time.

"Crazy. We're sitting here like a couple of shoe fetishists," Greta says. "I wonder what Dr. Winkle would say."

"They are museum quality though, Greta."

"You mean I shouldn't wear them, maybe put them in a glass case or hang them on the wall? Oh, I don't think so. He made them for me to wear, I'm sure. I think I should wear them. I don't want to be one of those people who save their quilts and heirlooms in a trunk and never see them, never use anything beautiful. Like Dorothy said, why wait for a trip to the moon?

"Mars, actually," Faun says. "I suppose." She reluctantly hands back the slipper. "You know, maybe his wife made them. Do you think?"

"Could be. No, a man made these. I just know it. My visitor during the storm. I'm sure, though I don't know why I'm so sure." Greta holds the moccasin away from her and lifts it up and down as if weighing the shoe. "Anyway, I'm thinking of adding a work room. On the lake side, with a big picture window. I was talking to Tom and he thinks I could have the big window if I use double strength glass."

"You'll have to put up dark bird silhouettes, like I do at the top of my A-frame, to keep the birds from crashing into the glass. They still do sometimes anyway. But it's a great idea," Faun says. "So you think the man with the long black hair made the moccasins?"

"I do," Greta says, slipping the moccasins on her feet. "I feel confined by the small pieces. I need to work larger–do some windows, actual windows, not only pieces to hang in windows. It's more natural, more traditional. And I just need to do larger pieces. Your outhouse window inspired me. I'll put my drawing table in the new room, and I want a chair like that moose antler chair over at Latos's Lodge. I'm going into town this afternoon to talk to Tom's cousin Otto, who's supposed to be a wonderful carpenter. He works with a builder over at Hornet's Nest." Greta can hardly wait for the room. It's going to be such a wonderful sunny room.

On the way home, Faun remembers the clipping she meant to give Greta, about *The Nutcracker* ballet in Winnipeg, with the rave review about that dancer, Gabriel Dimetri. But she decides, just as well she forgot. Greta would get the paper herself if she wanted outside news, and she always changes the subject whenever Faun brings up her days as a dancer. Whatever made her clip that out? Greta was so happy today. She speeds up, anxious to get started with the sheep dog wool she bought on their recent trip to Thunder Bay, humming to herself in anticipation. How little it takes sometimes, just a bit of sheep dog wool, a bit of elk fur stuck to a fence, or a new color, a new shade of yarn! Before she goes into the house, she takes down the fresh strands of golden wool hanging on the clothes line above the fresh snow. Yes, Christmas is wonderful this year.

Greta's Dream: A kitchen. She leans on the counter at Gabriel's. The counter is in Gabriel's house. He is in the kitchen, busy with something, but they seem to be at home together. Several bars of soap are lined up on the counter in a variety of shapes, all are clear glycerin soaps in attractive colors—red, amber, blue, pale green, lavender, clear, even black—they seem like large jewels. Gabriel says they are his Christmas presents and Greta feels bad at first because he got nothing but soap. Then she realizes, it's because he always looks so clean, something about his clean-looking face. Or is it because he's dead?

Chapter 10

The performance went well. Now Gabriel can taste the garlic from dinner. His lungs ache from the icy air as he walks quickly to his car. He feels slightly ill. While the car warms up he rests his head on the steering wheel and swears softly to himself. He was happy to be dancing again, but it felt strange. Closing night, he joined the others, of course, and there was too much champagne, the Italian food heavy with cheese, and the news about his old friends is making his head ache. Jerry, Antoine, Margaret. Tony in New York. AIDS. Gone. Dead. He can see them, their healthy bodies, the flush of their skin, the sound of their laughter as it echoed in the big dance studio. He feels their absence in the stillness; in the cold.

Someone taps on his windshield, concerned. Gabriel smiles to show he's okay, and waves the man on. He watches the man walk down the street huddled up against the cold in a bulky fur coat like a bear in black boots, until he disappears around the corner of the Hudson Bay Company. Gabriel slips Gould's final *Goldberg Variations* into the tape player, and heads North with his ghosts. He drives on automatic pilot, trying to ignore his nausea, but he is sweating by the time he gets out of town. He has to keep driving. The road is rough, his tires need air, and the constant vibration is turning his brain to mercury—heavy, smooth, and too susceptible. No one could tell him about Greta. They had heard nothing of her. But no one said she was dead, like the others.

The light is on at Dave's Service Station. Gabriel pulls in, parks to the side of the garage, and walks carefully inside, sees no one, and sits down on an orange plastic chair. He calls out "Dave," realizing he sounds like a sick wolf as soon as he hears his own voice howl out the name.

Dave comes in through the inside garage door, wiping the grease from his hands on a plaid flannel rag.

"Just finished. You're sick, Gabe," Dave says, walking over to him. He leans down for a better look, looking directly into Gabriel's pale face. Gabriel is too ill and tired to lift his head.

"Right," he says. "Can't dive. Drive. Champagne."

———

On his way home Dave drops Gabriel off at his house and sees him safely inside. He can ride down to the station with him tomorrow to pick up his car. Dave drives along the dark road with the satisfaction that they're more or less even now, and he can forget about the time he was such a drunken fool, after he and Tia broke up. Gabriel is a good man, not too bright sometimes, and a little odd, but a good man, he tells himself, rather pleased at Gabriel's overindulgence, though he hopes he's not getting in with a bad crowd down in Winnipeg. This never would have happened before. He never drank before, or maybe just a little wine once or twice a year. But when Gabriel was sick and he had to stop the car and they saw those deer, Gabriel cried out "Antoine," and reached out toward the deer like it was a personal friend, and that bothered him. And who's Greta? He kept asking where she was, he kept saying "Greta." He'd better ask tomorrow. Or maybe not.

It's just after midnight when Dave pulls into his driveway, relieved to be home these nights with all the deer on the roads. After closing the garage door he hears an owl in the woods. He stands and listens to its long slow hoots before he goes inside. That'll be one to start on, a good one to record with his new microphone. Maybe tomorrow night.

Dave grabs his notebook, goes straight up the stairs and climbs out the window to check the sky. He checks the time, makes his notations, props up his new birch pole marker and climbs back inside.

Despite the grease, he decides to shower in the morning. He doesn't mind the grease–he can smell it all over himself, even his hair feels clumpy with grease. But he's too hungry to wait for breakfast so he opens a beer, slices a couple of big wedges of Jarlsberg, and saws off two pieces of rye from the round loaf he picked up at Tia's store. He slathers on mustard and eats at the counter like a hungry giant, taking big tearing bites. Putting away the cheese he looks at the salami, thinks about taking a big bite, but slams the refrigerator door instead. He just might go on that moon walk next Monday. Tia says they usually have about seven people or so. He pulls the crumbled paper out of his shirt pocket.

JOIN US–ENJOY THE FULL MOON
on our monthly walk around Loon Lake.
Meet at the Northern Natural Foods Store
at 7:45 pm for hot cider.
We'll leave for Loon Lake at 8:00 pm.

He leaves the notice by the phone so he won't lose the details. Tia didn't seem to think it was odd that he was interested. When she was talking to her friend Snow Bird, they both acted like it was perfectly natural he'd want to come. Dave goes to bed feeling hopeful, tired, and smelling like the engine of a car.

———

The next morning, Gabriel wakes to the sun in his eyes. He shifts to his side, amazed at how good he feels. No headache. Nothing. He had a dream about Greta, but he can't remember what it was about. But he feels terrific. He lets himself wake slowly, and looks at the snow crystals in the lower panes of the window. Each one different, each perfect. How he missed his icy windows when he lived in Paris. He gets up, stretches in a sheath of sun, and looks out over his orchard down below in the snow. Trying to remember his dream, he catches a glimpse–sees Greta stretching at the barre before class with the sun shining across her hair. But he can't remember more. Out his bedroom window, a few sienna-colored apples still hang in the tree tops waiting for the crows and squirrels. Next spring he'll dance in the orchard. He says her name to himself: Greta.

He's squeezing the last few drops of juice out of a pink grapefruit directly into his mouth when the phone rings. It's Dave, who says he'll pick him up so he can get his car at the station. He tells Dave he's sorry he has to go down just for that, but Dave says he's taking down a part for a van he has to finish up, and that's why he was working so late last night–he towed a van full of rock musicians out of the ditch down by Half Crow Creek. He was working on the clutch last night and had the one part in his garage at home so he'll finish up this morning. They need it by noon. Gabriel is glad Dave doesn't mention his condition last night.

On the way to the service station Dave counts hawks.

"Seven," he says. "Another one on a fencepost. How the hell do they photograph something like that? If you stop the car it flies away. So even if you have a zoom lens it's flying by the time you're ready."

"I suppose you have to sit there and wait," Gabriel suggests. "Like for ducks. Build yourself a sort of blind."

"Hmm. Funny how you see so much more, once you start looking," Dave says. "Like those red dogwoods along here. Against the snow, who'd believe anything could be naturally that red. Of course it's only red in winter–turns dark in summer. I wonder why. Indians use dogwood for tooth brushes. Try breaking off a branch sometime. Keep twisting until it comes off, back and forth, you'll see why they use it. Yah, try it when you're out camping down on the lake."

"Have you ever been up to Churchill?" Gabriel asks. "To see the bears? Take pictures?"

"Funny, every now and then I think about going up there, but I've never been. I could have gone as a kid, but I had measles or something, so I missed out. I think I'd rather see a black bear. You'd have to be careful, taking a picture of a bear," Dave says.

"I guess," Gabriel laughs. "They can run like the wind."

"I can record them now too. Those hippie kids gave me a microphone, so I wouldn't call the police. Plus I made them pay me in cash, the balance due today when they come to pick it up. Bobbie, the one with the blue hair showed me how to use it. He had a suitcase full of adapters and stuff and fixed it up to my radio/tape player out in the garage. It records. I hadn't even known that. He had me hold out the microphone to the back of that old Ford out there that needs a muffler, and it recorded just like it sounds. Here we are."

The guy with blue hair is waiting in a black pickup when they pull in. He has a neon blue Mohawk, and an earring that looks like a screw in one ear. He pulls on a black beret when he gets out of the cab, and looks almost normal. He's wearing an expensive wool topcoat, and high black mukluks with leather lacing.

"Bobbie, this here's Gabriel," Dave makes the introduction. Dave is surprised that Bobbie knows Gabriel's last name. Bobbie tells Gabriel they all saw him, he and his band, in *The Nutcracker*, and that he is a great artist.

As Gabriel walks toward his car, he hears Dave

asking Bobbie how to record the great horned owl in the woods by his house.

———

Gabriel drives to his studio. He picks up his mail and the newest batch of notes slipped under his door.

His old films are ready. He can pick them up any weekday morning at the Northern Goose Photo Shop. There are clips of rehearsals, some quite old, from when he was still a kid, some from school, summer workshops, and later shots from his professional years. Winnipeg, New York, Copenhagen, Tokyo, Paris. His friend Juliette had done a montage as a professional project when she was at the Sorbonne. He found it last fall when he was cleaning the basement, but it was on 16 mm and he had no equipment to watch it. Now he can see it on DVD. He can't even remember all of what's on it. Maybe Greta?

Gabriel strips down to his tights and t-shirt and puts on his ballet slippers. Debussy's *Afternoon of a Faun*, or *The Firebird*? *Firebird*, he decides. Debussy would make him too sad; he's melancholy enough. Friends far away. Dead friends. Lost friends. He feels as he did with the migraines, but without the physical pain. He sits in the center of the studio and closes his eyes, trying to center himself, so he can dance, perhaps dance himself back into some light. How has he come so far since morning?

Jennifer opens the heavy old door to Gabriel's studio as quietly as she can, which is difficult. She has to hold it with all her strength to keep it from slamming in the updraft. She eases it closed, brushes the snow off her shoulders, and takes off her hat and gloves. She can hear *The Firebird* from the studio above, but he's not dancing. She waits for a loud section, then hurries up to the first landing and slides onto the window sill next to the radiator. She loves this wild music and forgets that she only stopped by for a moment of spying. She runs up the stairs and knocks on the studio door.

"Oh, Mr. Perez, I don't know why I'm here. Well, yes I do. I had to see you. Have you been crying? No. But you're eyes are just red. I'm always crying. It's my artistic nature. That's what Richard says. He's a senior. He's Rogers in the play. The butler. Will you come see it?" she asks.

"I'd like to. *Ten Little Indians*, yes. By Agatha Christie. I remember some controversy about the name. Good that they changed it. Are you in it too?"

"I am. I'm the cook, Mrs. Ethel Rogers. It's a week from yesterday. Opens Friday night, the 21st. You can come Friday night, Saturday night or there's a matinee on Sunday. I like this music, it's *so* dramatic."

"Stravinsky's *Firebird*" Gabriel says.

"*The Rite of Spring* guy, I know. Well, I have rehearsal now. I'm off. Let me know when you can come. I'll get you a ticket. I'm so happy, Mr. Perez," she says, backing down the stairs. She throws Gabriel a kiss and puts on her hat.

At his studio window, he watches Jennifer run down the street until her pale blue parka and bouncing white hat disappear into the snow. Greta had a white hat, furry like that, like a cat or a rabbit, and soft. What if that had been Greta, the other day when he was in Winnipeg? He had walked along the street toward his car and spotted a woman who looked like Greta. Partly it was the way she walked, so light on her feet, even in winter paraphernalia, that made him dash across the street. He was sure it was Greta. Or that it might be. He was excited, rushing along the street to catch up. But no, it was a pinch-faced woman with a scowl who clutched her purse to her chest when he caught up to her. She snorted at him and took off in a huff, her nose high in the air. Gabriel had felt empty as he watched her walk away.

Now he takes his time peeling an orange while stretching his right leg at a 90 degree angle against the smooth metal of the wood-burning stove. He switches legs while he eats the orange segments. All this mail. Every day more mail. Invitations, congratulations, long hand-written letters from students who want to study with him, some enclosing photos, today one with a DVD, letters from dance teachers who want to work with him, upcoming summer workshops; all the old possibilities.

He sets aside the mail and plugs in his camera which has needed recharging for months. He's filmed his students very few times in the last five years. They are uncomfortable watching themselves and become clumsy as soon as he gets out the camera. If they know ahead of time that he's filming half the class doesn't show up. The last time, which must have been late summer, Jennifer sat sobbing to herself in the back of the studio. They're too emotional. Or too young. Maybe he hasn't gone about it right. But lately he's been using it for himself, and finds it a helpful tool. One simply has to be objective and not take one's physical self too personally.

He can't remember a time when he wasn't objective about himself. He always observed himself. Back when he was very young, before he had even learned to speak, he recalls watching a butterfly in his backyard flying from flower to flower. It landed on his arm, and he watched the butterfly for what seemed to be a very long time, and that image has always stayed with him. He has a sense that he is something like that butterfly, something small and fluttery that exists whether you can see it or not. He's never taken his body personally, has never blamed it for the migraines, doesn't give it all the credit for his physical pleasures, as a dancer or otherwise.

His past lovers. All good. Funny how only recently he's realized how much they all resembled Greta, especially Juliette, whose eyes were as dark and brown as coffee beans. Greta's eyes were larger though. And they both liked poetry. He had liked to listen to Juliette read poetry in the bath, her beloved Mallarmé or Rimbaud. And he was sure she read whether he was there to listen or not. She would slip underwater mid-sentence and the poetry and Juliette would appear to drown, then bubble up moments later as a happy rippling laugh, and she would abruptly finish the poem in great seriousness. He sees her name in the credits of French movies now and then, as art director or montage editor.

Greta liked to recite poetry too, but she would do it from memory. She said she used to read poetry when she was little, when she was lonely and she just seemed to remember the poems she liked. And she used to write little poems, sometimes making them up as they walked along the river–short little poems about the birds or the sky or the rain falling on the treetops. He wishes he could remember the one about the rain. They were like Haiku, those short little poems she'd make up on the spot. She had a musical speaking voice and she spoke slowly, because she liked the sound of the words. *Rain.* He can just hear her say the word rain. *Rain falling down.* He might find her again. He might. Anything is possible. Now that he's dancing again.

What to do, what to do, he chews at the thick white pulp of the orange rind. Does he need to do anything? He's sure it would be easier if it were summer. It seems hard to think, with all the ice and snow. If he could get to Apollo Bay. But couldn't he? He could snowshoe, or hire a dog team. Dave will know someone with huskies, he's sure. He'll check after his acupuncture this afternoon.

PART 2

Chapter 11

Gabriel slows down as he nears the station, then speeds up again since it's obvious Dave has finished for the day and closed the garage. He is more determined to take a trip down the lake since his acupuncture session. He told Dr. Saunier about his lake idea, although he didn't tell him about the "spiritual migraines." Paul gave him a packet of loose green tea as a gift, and told him to call him at his office if he goes or leave a message with Trina as to when he'll leave, so he can chant and meditate for him. When Gabriel looked at him with concern at his comment, Paul simply laughed and patted Gabriel on the arm and told him: "It's fine. It's all part of it. We all have to live our own puzzles, don't we?"

Gabriel has seen Lake Superior's shore in late fall, cracked into great puzzle pieces of ice floating on the dark water and sloshing about like stranded ships. He's felt the winter winds cross the lake with a force a grown man has to brace hard against, and cold enough to make you forget your destination. He thinks of the steam he saw rising above the water last year before the freeze and the layer upon layer of gray–land, steam, sky–all one. Then the dazzling winter light of December on the white land. But he's only seen it from shore, he's never walked out into it, into all that white.

Gabriel knocks on Dave's door, and nearby birds fly off to the woods. No answer, and the door is locked. He goes around to the side, which is open. He steps inside and is startled by the unusually strong smell of burnt wood. One gray sock and a wood-burning tool hang from the clothesline strung above the wood-burning stove. The kitchen table is covered with newspapers, and Gabriel smiles at Dave's newly made wooden sign: "Dave

Duckett's Satellite Tracking Station." He's used the wood-burning tool to form the words, plus a constellation of the big dipper in the corner of the sign. He looks for some paper so he can write Dave a note. On the back of the moon walk notice by the phone, he writes:

Dave,
I've gone to Apollo Bay. I'll be fine and will call when I get back. Nice sign. – Gabriel.

That settles it. The note makes it final. He drives home, calls Pearl, his accompanist. He leaves her a short voice mail message to let his students know he's canceling classes for the remainder of the month and that classes will resume again in February. He remembers to ask her to tell Jennifer that he'll try to make it to the play if he gets back in time.

Next he gets out the Winnipeg yellow pages and puzzles over how to look for dog teams. He calls an outdoor sporting goods store and they call someone from the back of the store who knows someone. He takes down a number for a man by the name of Buckshot Johnson. Gabriel considers the name, pauses, then dials with determination.

Ghost Barns

Dave loves the sound of the wind blowing through the empty barns in the countryside. He and Bobbie with the blue Mohawk are in the middle of a barn adjusting the sound on the recording equipment. This is their second barn of the day. The first was an old wooden barn and now this one is stone, a thick stone barn built by a Scottish stonemason who built a number of stone houses in the region some years back. All excellent stone houses, built to keep out the cold and to last many generations, with fifteen inch thick window sills, the same as this barn, which is temporarily out of use. For Dave, it's a ghost barn. He likes to visit the empty barns to listen to the wind, and now with Bobbie's help he's recording the winter winds as they howl through the barns. They're getting a deep-toned cave-like sound from the stone barn. The first barn, an old wooden one, had a more whistling sound. They've also recorded flapping pigeon wings up in the rafters, and the cry of a scrawny cat, which Bobbie plans to take home if they can catch it–they almost caught it when they first arrived. In the wooden barn they recorded a shutter knocking back and forth in the wind, a creaking hay mow door, and now they're both startled– what luck, a cooing mourning dove. After they've recorded the mourning dove, Bobbie tells Dave to talk into the microphone and say "End of Ghost Barn Number Two," give the time and date, and tell a few details about the barn's history, appearance and location. Dave is enjoying this.

Chapter 12

Greta is in the kitchen sitting in her moose antler chair for the first time. It's very comfortable and quite throne-like, and she feels herself relaxing in anticipation of the animal wisdom she hopes will come from the chair. She plans to have only the chair, her red Rya rug, and a large plant in the new room. And of course the white drawing table and the cutting table, plus the work bench. She'll have built-in drawers for supplies. But she has to wait until the ground thaws before they can even start on the room. In the meantime she must be patient, even though she is already psychologically in the new room, facing the lake, absorbing the brightness of fresh snow, meditating through the icicles hanging from the roof, watching the snow blow across the lake.

Ice is becoming increasingly important to Greta. Each morning when she feeds the birds she breaks off an icicle from somewhere–this morning from the garage where the clearest and longest were reachable. She puts the icicle on a white serving dish in the center of the table where she can enjoy it while she has her toast and tea. Each one is different; each icicle melts in its own way. She loves the striations of air in the center of an otherwise clear icicle. Some have perfect little bubbly scenes, others the extreme clarity only ice can have, and perhaps glass. She's seen this iciness in glass.

She lets the phone ring while she finishes the last piece of toast and honey. She doesn't mind the ringing, and her friends know she doesn't rush, but she is surprised that it's Karloff. He rarely calls. He wants her to stop at Tom's before she comes over to skate, to pick up a gun. Tom's cold is worse and he's not coming to the sauna tonight. Sure, she'll pick it up, she tells him, though she's puzzled. Doesn't he have a gun? She remembers seeing Karloff last partridge season standing out near his dock, oiling a gun, or doing something with it as she paddled by. She's sure of it, yes, it was that last really warm day when she canoed down the lake to sketch lily pads. Maybe it wasn't his gun, maybe he borrowed it. It seems odd, in any case, since everyone on the lake has a gun, even she has one–a 22 she keeps locked in the built-in gun case in the back room of the cabin. There's room for five more guns in the case, so she keeps her old ballet slippers locked inside, though she doesn't really know why.

Greta plans to spend the morning working on Dorothy's fruit design. She can pick up the gun just before she goes to Karloff's. Last night she re-cut some of the leaves to replace the ones she chipped, and the new leaves turned out well, very well. She's using antique green glass with subtly mottled shadings and it was a stroke of luck how the darkest green had edged the leaves. She bought a considerable supply of antique glass in Thunder Bay at the co-op, left by someone who had given up on the art and moved to Vancouver. Ordinarily Greta has been intimidated by antique glass so hasn't given herself much of a chance to work with it, but her cutting has improved considerably in the past week simply by working with it.

Settling down at her work table she adjusts the light and starts fitting the pieces into place. The oranges and lemons fit like rising moons and suns above the deep purple cluster of grapes. The leaves she cut last night are undoubtedly the best curved work she's ever done, even though the shading was accidental, and now the leaves of the grape vine swirl around the fruit in a casual elegance. The background of this circular work is a cloudy pale blue. Greta tapes the pieces into place with infinite care, losing track of time as she works. This is the most enjoyable part of designing in stained glass–seeing all the pieces together for the first time, seeing it in glass. The taping takes time, and is a labor of love for Greta; the blooming of the garden. She knows this is one of her very best pieces, and decides to leave it as it is on the table. Enough for one day.

She stretches her arms high above her head, touches her toes, and stretches up again, celebrating her good health and the success of the morning's work. She turns up the volume of the music–Mozart's *Piano Concerto No. 20*. Faun keeps pressing her to get a CD player for the new room. Maybe. She has time to think about it, and if she goes to the glass show in Winnipeg next month she might look. Just so she doesn't end up like Faun who has music on from morning until night, and you never hear anything else. She always has a great variety of birds at the feeders on her deck, but you can never hear them.

Gabriel has been hiding lately, she doesn't know why. She's been sleeping again without having opened the bottle of sleeping pills, and she has little concern about his disappearance. She knows he'll be back–in the next snow, if not before. No use making a big deal of it, that was her problem before, she's decided.

The icicle is now the size of a small tooth. She pours it into the sink with the ice water and jots down on the calendar how long it took to melt, along with her comment of the day:

The longevity of icicles is always surprising.

She reads over the week's comments:

Monday: All is water. Rose-breasted grosbeak.

Tuesday: Also all may be ice. Skating.

Wednesday: My tea is made from the same water the dinosaurs once drank.

Thursday: Nothing is more beautiful than ice, except to dance.

Friday: Remember vanilla, almonds and oats. Circles.

She's on her way to Karloff's and the gun is in the trunk. She gave Tom's wife a loaf of banana bread when she picked up the gun. Efrozinia. An odd name. It's never seemed like a real name to Greta. Efrozinia, or Frozi, is Ukrainian and speaks only a few words of English, and once in a while she comes to a sauna evening, but Greta thinks it's only to please Tom. Tom calls her Frozi. Frozi is a large woman, not at all comfortable with her big rosy body. She's an alcoholic who knits in the mornings, when she's still sober. Faun buys wool for her in Thunder Bay and has been encouraging her to sell some of her mittens at the co-op. Last summer Faun brought her a notice of an AA meeting in Red Otter, but Frozi hid every time Faun stopped by after that, and wouldn't see her at all for six weeks.

Sometimes Frozi walks down the road to Greta's and gives her a present–a pair of knitted socks or mittens, and once, through much negotiation with Tom, Frozi took a boat ride down the lake with Greta to pick blueberries. They went down the lake to Sad Man Falls one clear summer morning and Frozi took her gray Persian cat along in the boat. She and the cat sat together in the bow of the boat like Queen Nefertiti and her palace cat, sailing on a pleasure cruise down the Nile of Life–that's the exact phrase that came to Greta that day, riding down the Nile of Life. They picked several quarts of berries while the cat wandered off, but later reappeared nonchalantly at the boat when they were ready to leave.

Greta thinks of Gabriel's mother sometimes when she looks at Frozi, though the two look nothing alike. Gabriel's mother was from Leningrad and a woman of high culture, quite unlike Frozi. Sometimes Greta gets angry thinking of Frozi and her drinking, her reclusiveness. Still, she knows getting upset about Frozi is like getting angry with a cat. Yet it's just such a waste, all that drinking, all that loss, even though she doesn't know what might fill its place. She drives past the hazelnut thicket where she saw Frozi picking nuts last fall. She had smiled as Greta drove past. But when Greta came back with a bag and walked off the side of the road to join her, Frozi ran off, cutting through the woods toward her cabin like a scared rabbit. So Greta picked the prickly hazelnuts by herself and spread them in the basement to dry until Christmas.

———————

Greta hears barking inside as she knocks on Karloff's door with the gun slung over her shoulder. Karloff shuts the door behind him and comes out to the porch to put on his boots. He takes the gun from Greta and they start down toward the lake.

"It's that Shadow, you know. I've got him now. Latos gave him up. The wolves–they come around, so I need the gun."

"I thought you had a gun," Greta says.

"It's no good. Bent."

That ends that, though she can't imagine how a gun would get bent. In the ice house they go through their skate lacing routine. Greta holds the worn eyelets on Karloff's skates, one pair at a time, starting at the bottom, while he pulls the laces tight, then he returns the favor on her figure skates. They do this with the patience and kindness of a brother and sister.

With skates neatly laced, they step awkwardly through the snow and out to their beloved ice. It's an ordinary cold evening, with little wind and many stars. Greta wonders if Karloff ever counts how many times he circles the rink. She never does, but she used to count laps when she swam in swimming pools. She doesn't ask Karloff if he counts, but estimates they do about fifty turns around the rink in an average evening. As usual, they finish at the same time, so tuned to one another slowing down, to the final circle. She knows he was waiting for her to do a spin, but she's not up to it tonight. Karloff's eyebrows and moustache are white with ice particles and she senses his heart isn't in his skating tonight either. She waits by the snow bank near the ice house for him to finish his last round. That's when she sees them, just beyond the far end of the rink. They hadn't made a sound. As he glides in, she points. Karloff picks up the gun and gestures her into the ice house. She hears one shot as she sits down on the bench of the ice house. Karloff comes inside and they take off their skates as if nothing had happened. It was a pack though, a pretty good-sized wolf pack.

Later, at Latos Lodge, the sauna group is sitting in front of the fire listening to Tom tell his wolf story. When the cuckoo cries, Tom pauses, sitting back while the bird counts off the hours. The others take good swigs of their beer and help themselves to more peanuts. At the closing of the cuckoo clock door, everyone leans forward again, their shadows forming a tepee from the light of the fire. So near the fire, Tom's face is as orange as a rutabaga in a Canadian sunset as he continues his story, having left off in the middle of the river when the cuckoo interrupted at nine o'clock.

"So I'm all alone out there. Only one fish in my creel. I've come, maybe a hundred yards down the river, standing in that wide pond—you know that place Latos, there's that little spring there, by those big red boulders. So I'm standing there ready to cast, and that's when I freeze. I'm just like some statue right there in the middle of the river. They're all looking at me. A dozen at least. Standing up on this ridge on the other side of the river. The big one in front is showing his teeth and rolling his black lips real slow so's I can get a good look. Then this big guy starts down the river bank real slow and I start backing away just as slow, walking backwards in my waders, hoping I don't trip. I'm reeling in the whole time and do everything real slow and careful. I make it out of the river and get out my knife–it's all I have with me. And I keep walking sort of half forward and half backward to the road, knowing my car's pretty close, yet you can't imagine how far it seemed. Then I just keep walking like that, mostly backward, shaking like a leaf the whole way, my jaw stiffer 'en a dead moose. I never was so glad to get in a car and out of there in my life, I tell you."

Tom finishes his beer in one big gulp, relieved to be away from those wolves again and next to the nice warm fire. After telling Tom that was some story, everybody sits and looks at the fire, thinking about the wolves, wondering what they would have done, glad it wasn't them. Tom doesn't tell what Frozi said when he got back that day and how she made fun of his backing down the road with a hunting knife. "You think a little knife is going to protect you from a pack of wolves?" she had said to him in Ukrainian, which somehow made it sound even worse, even dumber.

"Yoo hoo, Greta," Faun calls out as she nears the dock. "What are you doing out in the cold?"

Greta looks at Faun through a piece of blue glass as she skis toward the dock.

"What are *you* doing out in the cold?" Greta says.

Faun's cheeks and nose are red from the cold and she takes long smooth strides up to Greta's dock.

"Let me see," Faun says, taking the blue glass from Greta's gloved hand. She scans the now-transformed horizon of blue and smiles.

"Here, try pink," Greta says.

Through a chunk of amber Greta looks at Faun viewing their world through rose glass. Faun snaps off her skis and settles down beside Greta on the dock and they contemplate the frozen lake through various colors of glass from the tackle box between them.

Inside, over tea, they discuss what everyone on the lake is talking about: wolves, and what to do about them. No one can sleep with their howling. Yesterday morning when Greta was at the dock Tom came over after he finished chopping wood, madder than hell in his own quiet way, so mad he took out the howling on Greta, lecturing her on how those wolves better quit pretty quick, Frozi cries all night–says it reminds her of Russia, and her pillow is soaked with tears by morning, and it better not go on one more night. Tom walked off, said he was going straight to Karloff's. Thinks it's that Shadow of his–says the dog's not normal and something better be done real quick before everyone goes crazy. Faun had talked to Millie and Tillie at the grocery store in town yesterday, and they definitely have the jitters, and Tillie said Mable has such bad constipation over the wolves she didn't get out to the cemetery on Sunday.

"Seems to me Latos is the one who should do something, instead of just giving Karloff the dog, or wolf-dog or whatever he is, he should have done something. I don't know what, but he's the one who trains the huskies and knows about dogs and wolves," Greta says. "I just don't understand what they want. They're not hungry, couldn't be, going by all the deer on the roads at night."

"Well, I'm used to them, finally," Faun says. "I slept just fine last night. I suppose we're all used to them, hearing them howl from across the lake, it's just that they come so close now. And I don't mind their tracks around the cabin, I would just like to know what they want. I love wolves."

Greta moves the icicle plate into the sunlight. Faun is

caught up in Greta's ice fascination, and is planning a large shawl for herself in whites, with interwoven metallic silver threads. It'll be part of her winter uniform, to go with her silver arrow earrings and her white hair. She'll use some of her more unusual wools and furs, including the English sheep dog wool, some good quality sheep wool, and bits of fur she's collected from fences on her ski outings, which include deer and elk, and possibly wolf. Greta compliments Faun on her idea of using several animal yarns in one weaving–the blend of prey and predator appeals to them both.

They hear a car come down the drive and both get up to see who it is. Freddy Box, with the mail. He must have special news, to be driving up to the house instead of leaving the mail in the box. He parks and walks hurriedly toward the cabin with long nervous steps, spitting into the clean snow before he gets to the door. A snuff man, he sucks the remaining spit into the side of his mouth and his face is in a half-sided twitch when he tips his buffalo-checked hat to the women and hands Greta her mail, which includes supply catalogs, and a post card of Isle Royale in an unfrozen blue Lake Superior, from Dr. Willie Winkle, and which Greta knows Freddy has read and will tell everyone on the lake about within the next half hour. But at the moment he's just as interested in telling them to watch for Latos and his dog team on the lake.

"He's going down to talk with some of the Cree folk, Carl Come-so-Far or Jim Nightman, down by the falls," Freddy tells them breathlessly. "About the wolves," he hollers on his way back to his truck. He backs down the drive jerkily. Greta is his last delivery of the day, and they listen as he speeds off down the road in his excitement.

The postcard from Thunder Bay says Dr. Winkle will be in Red Otter this weekend and will be staying at Farrelson's Bed and Breakfast. Faun and Greta look at each other.

"There is no such place," Faun says. "Unless Darrell Farrelson is renting out his back room next to the gas station, heaven forbid." Everyone knows that Darrell and his house smell about as clean as a half dead goat, and Darrell believes he'll die if he takes a bath. He tells anyone who'll listen about his brother, who lived in a small shack out of town, never bathed, and then when they took him away to a nursing home two years ago, the first thing they did was get him out of his long johns and give him a bath, and of course, Darrell says, he was dead the next morning. But Darrell does leather work and makes hand-tooled belts, with exquisite animal and bird designs, which he sells at a stand in front of his house in summer, and from his living room in cold weather. If he weren't so good no one would go near him. The belts have to be cleaned and aired for a few months before anyone can wear one, but it's worth it, that's how good he is.

"Does Dr. Winkle have your phone number?" Faun asks.

"No, I never put it on my business card, and that's the one I left at the co-op with my address. But it's in the phone book. I'll leave my answering machine on this weekend. I'm tempted to be out of town–go down to Winnipeg for a little shopping, go to the art museum, maybe see a play. But that would be cowardly."

"Immature," Faun adds.

They both read the postcard again. He wants to take Greta to dinner, and a movie.

"The coffee shop is open until 5:00 o'clock on Saturday, and until 2:00 o'clock on Sunday. We could have lunch there. Of course there's no movie theater," Greta says. "I mean I'll have to talk to him sometime."

"People from big cities can't conceive of a town existing and yet not having certain things, like a movie theater. I went through that when I moved up here. It took me a while to figure out that the bait shop also rented movies. And I kept driving around looking for a deli, and

79

a small theater–thought I might get involved with that again. We should think about starting a little theater company ourselves. Just start by reading plays."

"Well, that's something else again. Maybe in the lodge. Good idea, but it won't help this weekend. What if I invite him to the sauna?"

"No way. He'd get the wrong idea."

"Well I don't want to miss skating or the sauna. He'll have to entertain himself. I'm not the Red Otter Chamber of Commerce–we don't have one. And here I am feeling guilty and I didn't even invite him," Greta says, shaking her head.

"The dogs," Faun almost shouts. They both rush to the kitchen window in time to see Latos and his dog team rush by–the dogs, frisky to be out, leap ahead of the sled pulling Latos down the lake. Running beside the team, unharnessed, and easy to recognize because of his long legs and black fur and white face, is Shadow.

Shadow's Song

my others,
needing my others
my furs
fast legs
hurt
in shut up doors
my howling moon
my sad white night
running
running.

Meanwhile, in downtown Red Otter, Dr. Winkle pulls up to Don's Grocery late Friday afternoon. He's spent the last ten minutes driving up and down Red Otter's three-block long Main Street looking for Farrelson's Bed and

Breakfast, and has decided, though he's been told the place is on Main Street, that it's one of those more exclusive and private bed and breakfasts without a sign. He'll find out in the store.

Don's Grocery appears to be deserted. There is no one at the checkout counter and he sees no customers, but the store is filled with a strong aroma of freshly cooked bacon. He walks past the produce section, which consists of apples, potatoes, carrots, onions, beets, and two surprisingly fresh heads of iceberg lettuce. He walks down the canned-goods aisle and counts five different brands of sauerkraut, next to the dog and cat food. Around the corner past the cereal, he comes upon an attractive elderly woman seated in front of the meat counter, eating a plateful of crisply fried bacon.

"Can I help you?" she asks Dr. Winkle, with a lovely British accent. "Don's out for tea at the moment."

"Yes, please. I'm looking for Farrelson's Bed and Breakfast. On Main Street. I can't seem to find it."

"Mrs. Don chokes on her bacon, rushes behind the meat counter for a drink of water from the sink. Coming back, better, but a bit red in the face, she tells him someone must be pulling his leg, or he has some genuine enemies. There is no Farrelson's Bed and Breakfast, but there is a Darrell Farrelson who lives next to the gas station down at the south end of Main Street, who makes leather belts, but he'll find no bed and breakfast there. If Darrell Farrelson had a bed and breakfast, it would have to be called the Pig Sty Inn, she tells him.

"Seriously, that's no place to stay. Darrell Farrelson is the dirtiest man in the province, now that his brother's dead," and she laughs again, but with more control this time.

"Bacon?" she says offering him the last piece.

"No thanks, but I'd better go see the man. I did make a reservation," he says.

"Well, suit yourself. There's Latos Lodge out on the

lake. He might open a cabin for you, even though he's closed for the winter. No running water though."

"Thanks, most obliged. What did you say your name was?" asks Dr. Winkle.

"Didn't. Mrs. Don, though. Dora Don. And you are?"

"Dr. Willie Winkle from Thunder Bay. Pleased to meet you," he says, nodding toward Dora.

"Doctor, are you. I wonder if you might take a look at my bunion while you're in town." She wiggles her right foot, and looks at Dr. Winkle hopefully.

"Sorry, I'm not a medical doctor. Mental," he says, tapping his head, and winking as he backs down the aisle away from the meat counter. "Say Mrs. Don, Dora. Do you know where I might find some coal?"

"Oh they've got wood-burning stoves out at Latos. He'll have wood," she says.

"No, I just need a small amount, just a few pieces–for personal reasons."

"Well," she sighs. "You could probably pick up a little out next to the railroad tracks. They're on your way to the lake, just past the bridge. You'll have to dig down under the snow, of course."

"Thanks," he says and waves as he heads past the potatoes and out the door.

"Darrell Farrelson's Bed and Breakfast," Dora says, clucking to herself as she washes off the greasy plate. "Mental, all right."

Chapter 13

Dr. Winkle pulls up in front of the only house next to the gas station. He had noticed the house before when he was driving up and down the street, because of the rows of cornstalks in the small front yard. Dr. Winkle hurries up to the porch, curious about this dirty Darrell who makes belts. Maybe he can help this man. A sign on the porch says: "Darrell's Best Belts." The extremely small lettering is done on leather, which is nailed to a blue painted board, the words about ten times too small to be read from the street. A snowdrift on the porch covers most of a bentwood rocker, and several frozen cardboard boxes. Three metal springs stick out of the snow from an old easy chair. He can see a few bat-like flaps of dark green Naugahyde dangling from its arms. He hears a radio from inside the house. Someone is at home. Dr. Winkle knocks. A cat leaps down from the porch railing and butts its head into his calf, then circles his legs like it wants to wind up Dr. Winkle.

The door opens, releasing a blast of air from the tomb of the unwashed Darrell Farrelson, and Dr. Winkle steps back as the cat scoots inside.

"Can I help you?" asks a thin raspy voice from the dark interior. Dr. Winkle waits a moment for his eyes to adjust from the snow bright day to the dark form of Darrell standing before him.

"I'm Dr. Winkle," he says as Darrell solidifies into a perfectly normal-looking man in a plaid flannel shirt and jeans. He is quite thin, with a stubbly beard. The top half of his face is tinted green from a plastic visor which is a size too large for his head.

"Come in, come in," Darrell says, stepping back.

Dr. Winkle makes a decision to ignore the smell. He

steps inside and closes the door behind him.

"It's my cousin Lydia, found me for you," Darrell says. "I didn't think you'd come though. She's lived in Thunder Bay forty years. She don't like me too well, so I didn't think you'd come. But I got an extra bed–cat usually sleeps back there, the sun's on that bed most all afternoon so Kitty here likes it. I'll show you. Watch that litter box."

Dr. Winkle follows Darrell through the obstacle course to the back room to see the bed. He can't decide if the front room is more like a disorganized garage or a junk store, but he suspects there's more organization than meets the eye. He gets a glimpse of the kitchen on their way, and finds it surprisingly unmessy. Almost tidy. And there's no smell of garbage; the smells are more animal. Maybe if he smokes it won't be so bad.

"Care for a cigar?" Dr. Winkle asks.

"No, never smoke. Bad for the body," Darrell says as he scowls. He shakes a finger at Dr. Winkle as he's about to light his cigar. Willie blinks. "I'm real sorry, but I don't think I can have any smokers staying here. That cigar smoke gets into everything–you just can't get it out."

Dr. Winkle folds up the book of matches, indignant and baffled.

"They told me at the grocery store that I might stay out at Latos Lodge," he says, tucking his cigar back into its case. "I'd better call out there before it gets dark."

"Oh sure, he's got the dogs, Latos does. Sled dogs. Always has a sauna Saturday nights. Tradition, that is. Not for me though. Folks in my family's allergic to saunas. Baths too. Very dangerous for us. My brother died when they gave him a bath up at the nursing home. Wasn't a thing wrong with him except old age. They killed him, is what they did. Nothing personal, you being a doctor, but they did it to him, giving him that bath."

Dr. Winkle uses the phone in Darrell's workshop to

call the lodge. The phone is one of those sturdy black models made to last several lifetimes. It hangs next to a wall-long tag board hung with hammers, saws, scissors, knives, and various precision instruments–some very similar in appearance to his brother's forged-steel dental instruments. The phone continues to ring at the lodge. Willie sits down and looks at the thick ropy veins of his hand under Darrell's green banker's lamp. Darrell's heavy work table has two rows of boxes filled with bottles of ink, sponges, pencils, tool bits, shells, stamps, pennies, and the box nearest him–a cigar box, filled with golden butterscotch candies. He helps himself to a candy while he waits. The sound of the telephone ringing in a lodge at an unknown lake with no answering machine to cut him off pleases Dr. Winkle, and he feels himself to be in a new time zone–Darrell's. He stands and walks as far as the short phone cord will allow. The walls, with the exception of the tool wall, are covered with calendars, mostly of animals, birds, flowers, and sea life. He stands before August 1967. A young deer in a field of purple asters. White horses snort in a misty Irish meadow in 1966 next to the pale rose sea anemones of 1965. The hard butterscotch candy melts into small slivers in Willie's mouth. He hangs up next to the green Chevrolet of 1955.

"Darrell," he calls out. "I won't smoke."

Chapter 14

Buckshot Johnson's sled dogs run across the frozen lake to the music of Mozart's *Magic Flute*, currently Act I, Scene II, Tamino's aria to the lovely, but far off, Pamina. "Then she would be mine forever," a voice sings out across White Bear Lake as the sled glides along pulling Buckshot and Gabriel.

Buck is pleased with the new CD player his cousin from Two Harbors sent him for his birthday; it doesn't freeze up, not even at -30 degrees, and he doesn't have to turn tapes like he used to do. The dogs hated that pause; it broke their rhythm and it would take them 200 yards or so to get back in sync.

While they packed for the trip Buck told Gabriel how his dogs were brought up on opera and how many years ago he hooked up an extra set of speakers to the kennel so they could listen to "Live from the Met" on Saturday afternoons. He said his oldest dogs have heard every New York Metropolitan Opera broadcast for the last ten years. They never miss a Saturday, and when the season is over, he replays their favorites on tape until the next season begins, although sometimes he'll vary their summers with a little Schumann or Mahler. He wants each concert to be a special occasion for the dogs, so he makes them wait until the weekend, unless they're out mushing. They all have their favorites. Violet, his dominant female, loves *Carmen*, especially the third act. She also adores Mahler's *Songs of a Wayfarer* and often sings along in the upper ranges. One of the reasons Buck likes the afternoons for their opera, aside from the fact that it's the Met's broadcasting time, is that they listen better during the day. He experimented with evening opera and it simply didn't work. At night they howl, joining *en rondo*—one coming in after another, forming a chorus of rounds in the manner of wolves, and thus creating unique elaborations of the operas that were really a little irritating to Buck.

"They love to be sad though," he told Gabriel. "It makes them happy; that's why they sing." Buck is convinced they understand any human language whatsoever–Italian, German, Swedish, Spanish, French, anything. Gabriel has some doubts about that, but thinking of his childhood dog, King, he wonders who's to say what's going on within a fellow creature? Do we understand through the meaning of words or the meaning behind the words–the passion?

Buck said Blackie is partial to Wagner; that he'll run forever for Wagner. On long trips Buck likes to use *Der Ring des Nibelungen*, because Blackie inspires the whole team with his passionate, almost ruthless, enthusiasm. He has a real commitment to Wagner. Gabriel was moved by the story of how a trip home last year was nearly fatal when the tape froze in the last act of Siegfried. They were racing a storm, and though Buck blew on the tape, and into the cassette player, he could only get it to keep repeating the line *Was she only asleep? Was she only asleep? Was she only asleep?* until the tape snapped and he had to finish the opera himself, or at least up to Valkyrie's Rock, singing all the parts, in order to get the exhausted dogs home before they were lost in the blizzard. And he wasn't too bad, he told Gabriel with a bit of pride.

But it was Buck's grandfather who had the voice, he said. Back in the old days his grandfather sold 78 records to supplement his trapping, taking an old Ford all over Blue Lake Township selling records. He didn't sell many–hardly anyone had a Victrola back then, and he put in a lot of miles for each sale. He got to keep some of the records for himself. His favorites were the Caruso records, though he liked Fritz Kreizler well enough too. But Caruso was number one. Buck told Gabriel how his grandfather would put on his good white shirt on Sundays and listen to his Caruso records all afternoon.

After the grandfather's dinner he would take his chair and a thermos of what his grandma called "bug juice" down to the dock, and as the sun set, he would sing. Buck said he didn't like to be bothered then, so some of the kids who liked to listen would sit in his grandma's screened porch and drink strawberry pop and listen to grandpa sing to the lake. He told how his grandma would say,"You boys come to hear grandpa sing to the lake?" "Sure," they'd tell her and she would let them help themselves to the strawberry pop in the ice box. They had to split one bottle three or four ways, pouring it into jelly jars, then they sat out on the couch with the poky pine needle stuffing. They would get comfortable under an old red Pendleton blanket that smelled of pine, and listen to grandpa sing Caruso songs while the sky turned the color of their strawberry pop. Even today Buck says strawberry pop reminds him of the sunset on that lake, and if he sits quietly on a summer evening listening to the breeze blowing through the pines, he can sometimes hear his grandpa singing Caruso. Gabriel could pictures the scene and is sure he would have loved to sit and listen to Buckshot's grandfather sing to the lake.

As Buck told his stories, he had loaded the sled carefully, and considering all of the winter camping gear they have along, it's quite light. He said he never overloads a sled, but he won't take Gabriel to Apollo Bay unless he has everything he needs to survive. Gabriel had to get on a scale while he was wearing all of his outdoor clothing, including gloves and boots, and Buck weighed himself the same way, then weighed all of the gear, before deciding what to pack. Buck says he has a box of heavier items that he keeps hidden down the lake, and they'll stop to pick that up.

This morning, after they loaded the sled, Buck introduced Gabriel to the dogs, one at a time. The dogs were not particularly friendly, but they were polite. Gabriel thought they were preoccupied with the trip ahead. He met Tristan and Isolde from Blackie and Pearl's final litter, then Blackfoot, who always teams with Caruso, and behind them, Wolf and Rose. Rose is milky white, with a pinkish spot on her nose. Baby Carmen and Kiri are next to the sled, and out front for a double lead are the majestic Blackie and Jet, followed by Violet and Blue.

Gabriel is getting accustomed to the feel of the sled, of being pulled across the snow. The dogs seemed to be working hard when they first started out, but now that they're warmed up the sled feels weightless, and the dogs pull easily, almost effortlessly, letting the sled follow along almost as an afterthought, gliding over the snow-covered ice. Buck and the dogs and the sled, and to his delight, Gabriel, are all part of this winter team, all one, gliding across the great white lake to the music of Mozart, whose music takes on new white dimensions.

Gabriel's senses are keen and his face pleasantly cold, and his heart is wild. He loves being with these dogs who look like wolves, on his way to Apollo Bay on this sunny winter day. For the first time since they pulled out onto the ice, Gabriel knows where he is. Even in the snow he recognized the large boulders that mark the half kilometer point to Apollo Bay. Like Dave, Buck calls it Turtle Bay. The winter vista of snow and ice has altered Gabriel's sense of time and space–he missed the lodge he knows they passed quite recently, the lodge where he stores his canoe.

As Tamino and Pamina begin their trial through the tunnel of darkness, Gabriel considers his instructions from Buck. Don't leave camp without the emergency items: fireproof matches, wrist compass, dried food, and the pack Buck made up for him. Keep the orange flag up, stay active, develop a routine, chop wood in the morning. Goggles are good for protection from the bright glare and from sudden wind and snow storms. Keep an extra pair of gloves handy when ice fishing. Don't stray far from camp if it snows; if it starts snowing when he's out, build a temporary shelter before it gets dark, a snow shed or a pine bough shelter. Buck will show him shelter building techniques before he leaves him at the bay. And he has a booklet on winter camping he can read in the tent.

Gabriel hopes he can master the snowshoes, they seem so wide and foreign, like heavy duty spider webs. His cross country skis will be more useful. He already knows the Telemark technique from last year, having learned easily with his dancer's lithe, muscular body and superb sense of balance. He plans to ski on the lake and adjoining hills every day as part of the routine Buck recommends establishing.

His biggest fear is of freezing his feet, and he can't explain why he's willing to take such a risk, staying out here for four days in winter, except that he has no choice. He just knows he has to do it. Today it's a mild 10 degrees, and the five-day forecast is for continued mild weather for the next two days, with light snow possible, then colder weather expected to move in from the north. Just beyond the lodge, they stop and Buck goes into the woods to his hidden box, and returns with the fishing spear and other gear, apparently also heavy items, that he keeps out here. The dogs spring off to his "Hike" as soon as Buck jumps aboard. Gabriel's getting onto the lingo: "Hike" to get going. "Gee" for right, and "Haw" for left. He has some others too, but Gabriel hasn't yet caught what they are.

The opera ends as Buck turns the dogs into Turtle Bay, Gabriel's Apollo Bay. Has Buck actually timed this? Without the music the silence is noticeable, and he can hear the tree-like creaking of the sled as the dogs ease up at Gabriel's snow-hidden beach where he pulls up his canoe in summer. The dogs are breathing heavily, panting as they wait for Buck to come to them with water and the signal to rest. He can see their breath, and his own as well. Buck's red beard is frosted white and little icicles hang from his mustache. Gabriel thinks he looks at home out here.

While the dogs rest, Buck surveys the immediate vicinity for a campsite, and chooses a flat area just to the bay side of a big granite rock, open to the bay but protected by the rock on the west, and by pines to the north and east. Gabriel helps spread a large tarp on the snow, and helps Buck set up the alpine tent and move the sleeping bag and supplies inside. Gabriel leans the skis and poles and snow shoes against the rock. Buck puts up a second tarp for Gabriel to cook under, and fastens the tarp ends to birch trees.

"Now if this were summer we'd have to string your food up that tree to keep it from the bears," Buck says laughing.

"And the wolves won't bother you. They're curious creatures, but if you stick to fish, you won't have any problem. Come on, let's go cut a hole."

Buck makes a two and half foot circle in the ice with the ice auger, big enough around for the spear. Gabriel had thought they would use a narrow saw and it would be like cutting an eye for an ice-skinned Halloween Jack-o-Lantern, which takes a certain awkward pressure to make a curve because a blade wants to move in a straight line. But this is easy. They put up the small purple bottomless tent over the hole and anchor it in the ice with heavy stakes. Buck tells him to keep the hole open, he'll leave the drill in case he needs it. When they were choosing equipment, Gabriel said he wanted to try the spear—thought he could avoid the turtles that way, but Buck said they hibernate in winter. Gabriel was surprised then when Buck packed a pole, and also stopped to pick up the heavy spear. Buck brings the pole and red box of fishing gear, pail and dipper, down to the fish house, and Gabriel follows with the heavy three-pronged fishing spear, feeling a bit like the devil. Buck tells him to be sure to close the tent well–it's got to be dark or the fish won't come, and to remember to brighten the bottom of the bay by dropping down oatmeal or rice–both are in his supplies.

Back at the sled, the dogs look lively and rested. Behind them in a spruce thicket, Buck shows Gabriel how to break off pine boughs–push in and twist. He demonstrates. Gabriel tries until he's broken off two boughs, more or less correctly. Then Buck makes a quick pine bough shelter. For a snow shelter he says to find a protected snow drift and use a tree branch or your snowshoe to shovel a space big enough to climb inside.

"Don't get scared. That's the main thing," Buck tells him, but Gabriel knows that already. They head back to the tent and Buck watches while Gabriel lights the stove. He's glad he's learned some of these things from Dave. The stove starts, and Buck seems satisfied.

They put up the orange flag together, shake hands, and Buck tells him he'll see him in four days. Gabriel watches as Buckshot Johnson, the opera musher and his team start toward home to the opening overture of Bizet's *Carmen*. He watches until the dogs become small black dots on the lake, and as they retreat he feels like he's the last man alive on the planet Earth, an infinitesimal dot in a universe of white. A speck. An abandoned child. A God.

The night his parents died he walked down the Champs Élysées and sat on a bench, leaned back and looked at the night sky for a long time, so expectantly. His mother and father died in a plane crash over France–they were coming to see him dance *Petrouska* with the

National Ballet of Paris. His mother adored Stravinsky. She was bringing him a surprise, she had told him over the phone from London. He danced so well that night–the final performance, he had thought they were in the audience; didn't know he was dancing for ghosts.

He walks over the dog tracks and out past the purple tent. The wind has blown much of the bay snow away. Buck had said he would need skis or snow shoes most everywhere, but here the snow is wind-packed and hard over the ice. As a child his mother told him, always in Russian, if you are afraid, be afraid. Be everything completely. Embrace whatever you feel. Be alive, Gabriel.

He starts across the bay in his new mukluks and feels light and free. He laughs, and the dance begins–a dance to the snow, and his music is the wind whistling through the trees. He has an audience of one–a curious hawk in a winter bare Tamarack. After the dance Gabriel realizes he doesn't need four days; that he doesn't need anything, for as long as he lives. That's how good he feels. He has no idea how long he's danced, but he is breathing heavily, his heart is beating fast, he's perspiring and he feels glorious. He's alone out here but he doesn't feel alone. He felt like this with Greta once when they were alone together, just dancing. There was only the dance, and it was enough. Greta. Just saying her name seems right.

He stops at the purple tent and dips the long-handled plastic dipper into the hole in the ice. Buck said he drinks from the lake all the time and has never been sick, not once, but he left a filter pump and purifying pills for Gabriel to use, if he chooses. Gabriel drinks. Sweet icy nectar. He hangs up the dipper on a metal tent brace, closes the flap to the fish house, and walks toward his arctic tent–big enough to sleep two, his home for the next four days.

Closing the screen behind him he takes off his boots and hat, gloves and mitts, and unzips his jacket. He lies down on his back on the plump down sleeping bag and rests, listening to his heart beat, slower, slower, slow, louder, closer, so close he feels it could talk. His senses are sharp, perhaps too sharp. He feels plugged into a whole new system and he's the man on Mars, except he's on the Earth. He looks at the bright red material of the tent above him as if he's never seen the color red before, this miraculous tropical color red, bright as a gaudy red orange parrot, a squawking color.

"I've been born again," Gabriel says aloud. "I'm a born again something. What a wonderland. A man could go mad out here." He watches the sky through the screen door and listens to a crow outside–a parrot in disguise? He hears the raucous caw of the bird:

No one sees all this beauty and here it is every day, and now here you are to see it. –The Parrot Crow.

The sky begins to brighten from the early setting sun. The snow turns pink. What color? Something more subtle than pink. Rose, a shade of rose? Like Greta's rosy cheeks. He smiles to himself, remembering how she always looked like she had just come inside from the cold. So fresh and rosy. Funny, he still remembers some of the lipstick colors from that day in New York when he and Greta went shopping one late afternoon. He needed a razor and she wanted lipstick. She debated among Pink Pink, Petal Pink, or Aspen Rose, choosing Aspen Rose after much consideration. But all the colors seemed pretty much the same to him. She knew that and laughed, but not in a way that made him feel color blind or foolish. They had talked about how men's products were so often black, the color of darkness. And he's had black soap, black hairbrushes, bottles of lotions and aftershave, almost always in black bottles. Black, the color of mystery. Gabriel absently strokes his chin, remembering, and watching the sky's light leave the day. He closes his eyes.

Gabriel wakes with a start. It's cold and dark; he doesn't know how long he's been asleep. He was just going to fix tea after he closed his eyes for a moment—there was still some red in the sky when he fell asleep. He zips his parka and pulls his socks up to his knees and huddles his knees to his chest to warm himself, finds the flashlight in his small pack, and the lantern. He turns on the lantern. Buck said it'll heat the tent a bit and he should leave it on all night if he gets cold. He puts on the rest of his gear, and steps outside with the lantern. The moon is big and low in the sky—it's two days until the full moon. The call of nature tells him how cold it really is. He allows himself only a second to think of his warm home, his spacious bathroom, his whirlpool tub.

The little kerosene stove starts readily and he begins to melt snow for a cup of Dr. Saunier's green tea. He dumps in more snow as each half cupful melts to liquid, and he's happy thinking of Dr. Saunier wanting to meditate and chant for him; somehow he's certain he'll do so on the night of the full moon. When the snow water is hot he pours it into his tin cup with the tea ball filled with green tea, turns off the stove, and carries the tea carefully into the tent, not wanting to spill a precious drop. The warmth of the cup is nearly as satisfying as the tea. Gabriel has had enough green tea to appreciate the quality of this tea. He dips dried apples into the tea, and eats a handful of almonds and raisins, and with a few hard pepper crackers, he's satisfied. He would like to go outside and sit on the big rock and contemplate the moon and look at the stars, but decides to stay inside this first night, let his body adjust to the cold, and take advantage of the warmth he feels from the tea. He reaches outside the tent and dumps the leaves from the tea ball onto the snow, then closes the tent for the night, leaving a quarter of the screen window exposed for the moon light. If he turns the lantern off later on, it won't be completely dark.

He'll read for a while, then listen to music on his CD player. He prefers not to read and listen to music at the same time.

Warning Signs:

Shivering is a form of exercise which a person can keep up for hours. At some point the muscles tire and lose their ability to shiver. This is a certain danger sign. Hunching over is another automatic action the body makes in the cold and is a way to protect the internal organs. Persons found frozen to death are often found in a fetal position with their legs pulled in tight. Yet people have been found "frozen stiff" who survived with surprisingly few ill effects. Often, death occurs when the blood turns to slush and the red cells can no longer carry oxygen and thus the freezing person suffocates.

Safety on Ice:

After a lake is frozen and the temperature continues to fall, the ice may crack along the shoreline due to pressure. Deep lakes can remain open in the center all winter, while shore ice is risky, and the middle area between the center and the shore is the safest for fisherman. Don't forget that ice is lighter than water. Ice floats and water supports it. Each winter fishermen become trapped on ice which breaks away from the shore and floats out into the lake.

Enough. He puts the book in the corner of the tent and gets himself ready for bed, zips up his sleeping bag, and slips Glenn Gould's first recording of the *Goldberg Variations* into the CD player. The only other CD he has along is Gould's final recording of the *Goldberg Variations.* He'll save that for the full moon. Gould's

Bach is intimate, joyous. There are no distractions; no traffic in the distance, no humming refrigerator, no furnace noise. The piano has never sounded better than in the concert hall of this arctic tent.

The lamp casts a fire-like glow on the red tent wall and he decides to leave it on all night. As the *Variations* end he's feeling relaxed. Gould's humming lingers as a friendly afterthought and Gabriel feels surrounded and comforted by distant friends, but he ponders the odd dream he had after he danced, when he fell asleep so quickly, and unintentionally. He was standing on a wooden floor in a studio, with clear plastic cellophane wrapped around both of his hands, and part way up his arms, though you couldn't see it since he was wearing his sheepskin jacket and just his cellophane hands stuck out. He was trying to unwrap the dog, a white dog, somewhat larger than a husky, but short haired and very white. He had wrapped the dog in a clinging plastic wrap and it stood there patient as a saint, its face squashed against the clear cellophane. Gabriel wanted to unwrap the dog but he didn't know how, didn't know where to start. He was too confused, so he just stood there beside the dog, until she came to help. He couldn't see her face but she was kind and seemed to be a friend, someone he knew. He woke up before he found out who she was. And he falls asleep, wondering if mermaids could live under ice.

———————

Earlier the same day, and further down the lake, Jim Nightman is skinning a rabbit next to his dock when Latos and his dog team pull up. After checking on the team, Latos and Shadow walk over to Jim as he finishes stripping the fur from the very naked-looking rabbit, its pink flesh glistening in the sunlight.

"How's it going, Jim?" Latos says in greeting, and

Shadow moves his nose toward the rabbit and looks up at Jim, who holds his knife upright and shakes his head. Shadow steps back.

"Smart," Jim says.

"He is. Name's Shadow. He's the wolf hybrid that's driving everybody crazy. I let him run when he was a pup and now his wolf friends come visiting and howling. Very sociable with the wolves," he says rubbing Shadow's head. "He's got some real close wolf friends but I don't know as how he could live out in the wild. Don't know if some of them might kill him. I can't figure him out, to tell you the truth. I've never seen anything like it, the way those wolves come around and howl. I don't know what to make of it. Every heard of anything like that?" Latos asks as he ruffles the fur behind Shadow's ears, and Shadow watches Jim as intently as does Latos.

"Let's go in," Jim says, pulling the last of the white fur off the rabbit's back leg. Latos takes a pail of water down to the dogs, then joins Jim on his porch where he has several skins already stretched on a wooden rack—more rabbit, one ermine, and a couple of deep brown pelts. They hang up their jackets and leave their boots on the porch.

Inside, Jim hands the rabbit to his wife, Sara Blue, who smiles shyly at Latos. The house is made of hand-hewn pine logs, and the furniture is pine, all hand-made by Jim. The kitchen is the visiting room and the warmest room of the house and it feels wonderful to Latos after his long trip down the lake with the dogs. Latos and Jim sit at the table while Sara Blue cuts the rabbit into chunks and starts frying pieces in fat on the wood-burning stove. Latos can smell bread baking in the oven.

Sara Blue's current handiwork rests in a birch basket on a bench beneath the window. To Latos it looks like a buckskin shirt, or maybe a jacket, and he can see she's started a bead work flower pattern on one of the sleeves.

She keeps her beads, separated by color, in an old muffin tin on the window ledge. Latos has tried to get her to sell some of her handiwork to him in the past, but she says she can't. She apologizes and says it's not good enough so she can't sell it to him. But it's too good, he knows that. Jim says she's superstitious about it. She'll trade or sell him a quill-trimmed basket once in a while, but not the bead work.

They drink coffee in the blue and white cups Latos traded Jim for maple syrup some eight or nine years ago, the first year they met. They sit without talking for a half cup of coffee before Jim says, "It may be Shadow is a spirit dog." He tells how sometimes a wolf or a dog or a wolf dog, or any animal, can be a spirit animal. They're not like other animals of their breed, but have been sent as a teacher or to do magic. He says all animals can teach us about things, but a spirit dog is rare; any spirit animal is rare. He says there was a white deer once, in his great grandfather's time, and there were three bad winters when many of the animals froze and the people didn't have enough to eat, and then the white deer came and walked the hills at night, every night–they said it never slept. The white deer would walk night after night, all winter long, and that was the last bad winter in that region and ever since the people have had plenty to eat. The spirit deer went away the following summer, and has never been seen since.

They drink their coffee and listen to the rabbit sizzling in the pan.

"I want you to take Shadow," Latos says.

Jim is quiet, thoughtful. Finally he sets down his coffee cup and says he'll take him.

"His mother died of an infection, she and the other four pups–three females and one male. The pups were two months old when they died. Shadow was the only one who lived, but he was sick for a month after he was left alone. The father was a black wolf. I only saw him once. Maybe I'm asking too much?" Latos looks questioningly at Jim.

"You are, but I'll take him. If you come to me on this there must be a reason, some higher reason," he says.

"Sara Blue, you been listening? Okay by you?" Jim asks.

"Yes. I know that dog. One brown eye and one blue eye. Okay with me, but it's the dog who'll decide what's okay," she says.

"Thanks Jim. Sara Blue," Latos says, getting up from his chair. "I was hoping you'd take him. I've got a bag of food down on the sled. His collar too, and the leash, in case you want it. You might put it on him when I go. I have to get back for the sauna. Tom Hanson's starting the fire for me and I'm sure he'll do fine, though I have my own way I like to do it, and well, I need to get back anyway. You two are always welcome for the sauna, you know. Any Saturday night. You just come over anytime–stay over in one of the cabins–you just take your pick." Latos stands above Sara Blue's bead work in progress. "Who gets the fancy work?" he asks.

"That's for Angela Come-so-Far, Carl's sister," she tells him, glad he hasn't asked if he can buy it, so she doesn't have to tell him it's too poorly made. She smiles and they all go out to the porch. Sara Blue looks out to the lake while they get ready.

"Nice dog," she says when they leave the cabin, and Latos is pretty sure Shadow will soon be eating fried rabbit.

Leaving without Shadow is one of those funny things for Latos. He feels bad leaving Shadow behind. He patted him on the head but he couldn't look at him, and now he's ashamed that he's glad Jim took him and he doesn't have to worry about him anymore. His neighbors won't be hounding him about the howling. It's a confusing feeling, something like he gets when he chops the head off a chicken for Sunday dinner, but not as bad as shooting a wounded deer that's got a fawn inside, like he has to do sometimes when they get hit by a car. He just wants the dogs to take him home. The sauna will help. It always does.

The huskie team takes off smoothly and soon the sled and team are racing across the ice. A mile or so past Jim Nightman's, Latos spots an orange flag, and the corner of a bright arctic tent as they near Turtle Bay. He hadn't noticed on the way out. And someone is leaping around. Dancing, yes, my God someone is dancing on the bay; Latos can't quite believe what he's seeing as his sled nears Turtle Bay. The guy dancing doesn't seem to notice him. How does he do that? Latos puzzles to himself. He's never seen anything like it; the man is almost flying across the ice, yet he moves in slow motion as he leaps high up toward the sky like he's going to sail to the sun, then lands as easily as if he's a light-footed deer.

Before he knows it, they've passed the dancer. If things were normal he would have stopped as soon as he saw the tent, visited a little. Made sure everything was all right. But nothing about the day has been normal, and he doesn't quite trust what he's seeing now, actually wonders if he's seeing things as the dogs pull on. He assures himself it's okay for someone to be leaping about Turtle Bay like that, as long as they have one of those tents. Going by the unique red-orange color, it looks like one of those expensive arctic tents, good for way below zero and for high altitudes too. Could be someone from Winnipeg, or even Toronto, he tells himself. A different breed they are, but he'll call Carl Come-so-Far when he gets back, then Carl and Jim can keep an eye out for the guy, make sure he does all right out there. Or should he call? Maybe he really is imagining things. No, he saw him all right. What a day.

———————

Latos gets back to the lodge before dark and sees a white wisp of smoke above the sauna–to him, a smoke signal that all is well in the world. The dogs are still frisky and slow to calm down after the long run. They gulp down their evening meal as if they've been starved for days. He's hungry too; knows he could have had rabbit and fresh bread if he'd hinted, but he had to get back. Everyone counts on him for the sauna. He likes to think it is as important to them as it is to him, and hopes that it is. He watches Tom come out of the sauna and down the hill to the kennel road.

"How's your cold, Tom?" he asks as he shuts the door of the shed where he keeps his sled.

"Not too good. It's in my chest now." He stands looking at Latos for word of Shadow.

"Yah, Jim took Shadow. I think it's going to work out, but we'll have to wait and see," Latos says.

Tom nods his head. "Well, I'll tell Frozi," he says. "The sauna'll be ready on time as usual, but I'd better go home. I'll have a snort and just go to bed."

The two men stand on the road in front of the sauna, smoothing and rearranging the snow with their boots and Latos thinks about the dancer. He could tell Tom, except Tom has a bad cold. Maybe he'll talk about it at the sauna, tell the guys. He'd better not mention it to the women though, they'd think he was off his rocker. Course the men might too.

Tom's pain is gone now but this morning it really hurt–near scared him to death. It felt like someone hit him with the blunt end of an ax or a big chunk of ice, right in the center of his chest. He doubts it has anything to do with his cold.

"Latos," he says, unburying a pine cone with his toe

instead of talking about the chest pain. "Someone called the lodge this afternoon–let the phone ring about twenty times. I just let it ring, figured they'd call back. Well, I'm off now. See you," he says as he walks down the road toward his truck, and the crunch of his boots in the snow echoes the rasping within his chest.

"Thanks for the fire," Latos calls after him.

In the lodge kitchen Latos fries himself a thick venison burger and heats up leftover brussel sprouts in the microwave. The twins are bringing a hot dish tonight, but he can't wait that long. While the burger fries he opens a beer for himself in the bar and puts enough bottles of Moosehead, plus a few root beer and creme soda in the bar refrigerator, and sets out clean glasses on a tray. He'll put out a couple of bags of pretzels after he eats. He's so hungry he half bites his cheek, luckily just scraping it a little. His hands are trembling from hunger as he finishes his venison burger, and he drinks the beer too fast.

Thinking about the dancer as he rinses off his plate, he considers the possibility of UFOs, not that he believes in them. But say there was such a thing, now this part of Canada would provide excellent landing fields, especially in winter with all the frozen lakes. And someone from outer space may look just like an ordinary person, but might have unusual abilities, like that dancer. He looked pretty regular, from a distance, taller than usual though. Something familiar about him too. He didn't see any snowmobile tracks or other tracks, but he could have come from the other direction. Yet he hadn't heard a snowmobile all day. Latos pours himself another beer. "Probably from Toronto, or Mars," he says out loud and laughs.

By the time Karloff arrives, Latos is slouched back in his big moose antler throne, listening to "Yesterday" by the Beatles on the jukebox because he pushed the wrong button.

"Hey, Latos," Karloff says, walking across the wood floor of the big empty lodge.

"You here? Already?" Latos says, surprised to see Karloff. Latos has forgotten it's Saturday night; he's forgotten that years have gone by. Karloff pulls up a chair, and has a good look at his friend and sizes up the situation quickly enough.

"I'll get us some coffee," Karloff says and leaves to start the ten-cup percolator. He starts a fire in the fireplace while the coffee perks, knows Latos just needs someone to sit with him, get him through his slump. Happens now and then, though Karloff hasn't seen Latos so bad since his wife left for that professional bowler from Minneapolis seven years ago. He and Latos, and Tom's cousin, Otto, were putting a big screen porch on cabin no. 12, out on the point, the one they call the Honeymoon cabin, because you can only get to it by boat–there's no road. Latos thought he would have to put in at least a 4 WD road, but cabin no. 12 filled up first every year as soon as they started calling it the Honeymoon Cottage. His wife was gone when they got back from putting in the porch screens. She just left a note that said: "Gone bowling," and she never came back. Latos drank himself into forgetfulness that fall after the lodge closed.

Karl has made the coffee double strength, and after half a cup Latos has already straightened up in his chair and is almost presentable when the twins come in with their hot dish. Karloff gets up to greet them as they head for the kitchen to put the hot dish in the oven, on warm, as is their custom. He tells them Latos is drunk but that they should act like they don't notice, and he'll come out of it sooner. "Just go on as usual," he tells them.

"We've been doing that all our lives for one reason or another, Karl Karloff, don't you know that?" Millie snorts, surprising Karloff a bit.

"What's the hot dish?" he asks, to change the subject.

"Macaroni and cheese with raisins and artichoke hearts. We're experimenting for the church food fair," Millie says.

"For most original entree," Tillie adds.

"Well," is all Karloff can think to say, just as Greta and Faun come in the door laughing, letting the door slam behind them. "Yesterday" is still playing, or replaying on the jukebox and Faun and Greta start singing along. Karloff wonders why they're so jovial–thinks this is turning into a really strange day.

Faun tells everyone that she met Tom on the road and she honked so he would stop because she was concerned that he was heading home instead of to the lodge, and that he stopped and told her he was sick, and that Latos gave Shadow to Jim Nightman. "So that's it," she says, "at least for the time being." She asks where Latos is–he's slumped down into the past in his chair again. Karloff points, and says "He's tired from the trip down the lake."

"He's okay though?" Greta asks.

"Sure, he's fine," Karloff assures her.

Karloff is sure Greta and Faun have a big secret, but they're not about to tell anyone what it is yet. He doesn't mind, there's plenty of time. Canadians know how to wait.

———————

In the sauna the men are sitting on the middle shelf, instead of at the top, as they usually do. Karloff throws a dipper of water on the rocks, and sits back down in the steam. Latos, sitting between Karloff and Otto, is slicing through the steam with his hands, as though measuring and chopping the steam into two-inch sections. Karloff and Otto say nothing about his odd conducting movements, figuring the movement, as well as the steam, are getting the alcohol out of his system.

"Do you know anyone whose life isn't a tragedy?" Latos asks as he continues to conduct and slice the air, expecting no answer.

Otto and Karloff know enough not to answer. Otto gets up to get the switches of birch and hands a few to Latos and Karlos, keeping some for himself, then throws another half dipper on the rocks.

"Personal tragedy," Latos says, flicking the birch branches against his thigh. "Millions of them," he adds, reaching above his shoulder to flick the birch twigs against his back. For the next five minutes the men switch themselves lightly with the birch switches, casually, yet as if the sauna is swarming with flies. Gradually they slow down their switching, until they're sitting motionless as three red and rosy naked Buddhas with their ceremonial birch wands and big northern feet, silently meditating in the steam, transformed by the fire and water of the sauna, their spirits at peace, and most of Latos's alcohol and despair evaporated and risen up the chimney.

By the time they've rolled themselves in the evening's new light snow, and dressed, all three are recharged and Latos's faith in the all-purpose power of the sauna is confirmed.

They have reversed the order of dinner tonight, in order to eat after the sauna, instead of before, so when the men come inside the women have already placed two small wooden tables together cozily in front of the fireplace, set chairs on one side, and pulled a bench to the fire side. The table is covered with a deep blue cloth with frayed edges, and a rather too large arrangement of dried flowers and dusty pheasant feathers is set in the center. The men sit down on the bench in unison, and immediately get up again and push the bench aside and pull up more comfortable chairs. Tillie sets the creative casserole with raisins on the table. Faun has brought freshly-made Italian focaccia, baked with extra virgin olive oil and herbs this afternoon, and which she knows everyone but Greta will eat with Ketchup and Otto's homemade blood sausage which has been in the warming oven for the past half hour with the now slightly crusty hot dish. Millie has set out a glass of ice water for each person, and put extra glasses, root beer and creme soda, but no beer, at the end of the table. Faun tucked a bottle of Chianti she bought in Thunder Bay back into her old canvas Literary Guild tote bag, unopened.

Greta has asked Faun not to mention Dr. Winkle being in town, because she doesn't want anyone to know she saw a psychiatrist when she was in Thunder Bay, but Faun says she can just say she met him at the artists' cooperative where he bought the stained-glass work and they needn't mention the office visit at all.

Greta heads to the kitchen for pepper. It's still snowing and even from inside she can tell it's those amazing huge flakes that are so noticeably perfect, individual. She thinks of herself and her friends as flakes of snow, unique like that, floating through the night. Gabriel used to say our lives were so infinitesimally brief, if we consider eternity, that a life really goes by in the wink of an eye.

Greta returns to the table determined to enjoy a piece of Faun's Italian bread and some of the twin's macaroni and cheese. As long as she doesn't look at the red-black blood sausage she won't loose her appetite. And Mable came late and missed the sauna, but brought a raspberry pie which looks exquisite.

As they begin the meal, it's apparent that Latos is pretty much back to normal. He tells everyone about the trip down the lake to see Jim Nightman, and they're all pleased that Shadow has a good new home, and yet may have the option of going wild. They can't hear enough about spirit animals. Everyone is fascinated by the story of the white deer, and the possibility that Shadow might be a spirit animal.

Karloff says he wouldn't be at all surprised if he wasn't a spirit animal, being half dog and half wolf, and with those two different color eyes, you couldn't really look at him. Karloff's opinion is that he can go either way–he could be tame or wild, or tame half the time, and wild the other half.

"I think maybe I was darn lucky he stayed with me, even if it wasn't for long," Karloff says. "A spirit dog would leave some kind of magic behind, wherever he goes, I would imagine," and Karloff feels a real sense of luckiness, so much so that he can see the hair on his wrists stand up, as if there is too much static electricity around him.

Everyone has a tale to tell about Shadow, or some incident with a dog they've known, and with all the spirit animal talk, everyone seems to have forgotten the howling that was getting on everyone's nerves, until Mable reminds them as she cuts the pie. "I hope he don't come back," she says, passing everyone a large wedge of pie topped with vanilla ice cream. "He scared me."

They start eating silently, the pie is heavenly and they know it deserves their full attention. Latos doesn't want anyone to go home thinking about Shadow, so he tells them about Jim Nightman's wife, Sara Blue, and what a talented artisan she is and how she makes beautiful beaded clothing and bags and moccasins, but won't sell any of her work. Greta and Faun look at each other, and feel they know where Greta's Christmas moccasins came from. Greta asks if Jim Nightman has long hair, and is puzzled when Latos says no, it's real short and prematurely gray.

Latos shrugs his shoulders, thinks he shouldn't have brought up Sara Blue and her bead work after all. Now they'll be thinking about the break in when they were down in Thunder Bay. He doesn't know who that was–could have been anyone, as long as they had long black hair. Latos goes to the jukebox, and plays the Tennessee Waltz, glad the evening is over and he kept the dancer form Mars to himself.

The air outside is icy, no wolves or dogs are howling, and the pick-up truck doors slam shut one after another following hasty good-byes. Faun and Greta are the last to leave, and ride together in Greta's reliable old Volvo. There is nothing left of their silly frivolity of earlier in the evening, brought about by the telephone message Dr. Winkle left on Greta's answering machine which they both listened to.

"Greta? Dr. Winkle here. Willie, to you of course. Well, I made it. Call me when you get back. I'm at Darrell Farrelson's Bed & Breakfast–not quite what I expected, no, but I'm sure it'll be a worthwhile experience. Most interesting town, and Darrell has a lot of fine leather crafting tools here, and a remarkable calendar collection."

They slow down for the eyes in the ditch. Two does. Faun invites Greta to stop in for Chianti and stay over if she wants, and she eagerly accepts, being none too keen about going home now that she's thinking about the long black hairs on her quilt in December, and she doesn't want to find another message from Dr. Winkle on her answering machine, or him parked in her driveway. She can call him tomorrow in time to arrange a lunch at the coffee shop, and then she assumes he'll be leaving. Another pair of eyes shine out from the edge of the road, either a small fox or Frozi's cat. It darts into the woods as they pass by, and Faun is relieved to reach her drive without seeing any more eyes. From Faun's back porch she points out the moose prints next to the hay bales she keeps over her rose bushes.

"Like living in a zoo," she says as she opens the door, and they hear the far-off cry of a wolf as they step inside.

At Apollo Bay, Gabriel's eyes have adjusted to the dark inside the purple fishing tent. He watches the pale orange bits of bait float slowly to the bottom of the bay where he's dropped the oatmeal. Occasionally he sees a flash of tiny fish flutter past the ice hole but it's their enemies, the big pike and walleye, that he's waiting for. The spear is heavy so he doesn't actually have to do much. All he has to do is wait, then drop the spear when a fish comes into view. He likes that the weight of the spear will kill the fish, making him less involved than if he had to use a good deal of force to hurl the spear, but he knows spearing is luck–either his, or the fish's, and the larger fish are smart, which is why they are large. The timing is the critical part; he has to drop the spear at precisely the right moment, slightly ahead of the fish as it moves within range–its winter sluggishness will be to his advantage, yet it will lurch ahead as soon as it senses danger.

A sleek gray blimp of a fish glides into view and pauses momentarily. Gabriel jerks the spear over the hole, and the fish is gone. He moved too fast. He decides to hold the spear directly over the hole, then all he'll need to do is let go. He drops more salmon eggs into the water and a few pieces of marshmallow laced with rice to make them sink just a foot or two. He positions the spear with the tips just under the surface of the water. He's ready, particularly now that his stomach is grumbling. He's alert. The spear gets heavier as the minutes pass by. He keeps his eyes on the hole and hardly lets himself blink. When he's almost ready for a break to rest his arm, a large dark walleye swims into view, snaps at the bait and hovers directly below the ice hole, gobbling up the soggy bits of marshmallow. Gabriel drops the spear. A hit. The spear and the fish drop toward the bottom of the bay. As he hauls the spear up by the rope he feels a leaden movement–something passing between he and the fish like a deep unpleasant ache, similar to a deadened tooth being pulled out of its socket. Gabriel lifts the spear out of the water and the walleye writhes trying to free itself, but is held fast by the primitive fork, a prong deep in its head and mid back. The pike's mouth gapes open at the horror of its own death. Blood. Fish slime. The intricate pattern of silvery scales. Gabriel shudders as he pulls the fish off the spear and lets it slide into the pail near the tent's door. He swishes the blood off the spear in the icy water. The fish makes a last feeble slap against the bottom of the pail as Gabriel walks outside into the bright winter morning.

Coming out of the tent, he stumbles and nearly drops the fish when he sees a wolf standing a mere 20 yards from him. His first thought is to get his fishing knife out of its sheath. He hesitates. Is it a wolf? It's big and long-legged. A dog? The creature wags his tail at Gabriel, and makes a bowing gesture to show he means no harm; that he's friendly. Gabriel relaxes, and calls out to the wolf dog. "Here boy." The wolfish dog trots over and continues wagging his tail as Gabriel ruffles his fur. Gabriel laughs out loud; he adores this dog that looks like a wolf. And his eyes, such wonderful expressive eyes, one yellow-brown and one blue–an odd dog, yet he has great dignity. He sits beside Gabriel as he cleans the fish, and eats a small portion of the innards Gabriel tosses him, but appears to do so more out of politeness than hunger. He follows Gabriel about as he assembles his cooking equipment and gathers twigs and pine cones to use as kindling for the fire. Gabriel wonders if the dog watched this morning while he cut a fallen birch tree into logs, or if he was nearby while he did his morning exercise routine, as best he could in bulky winter clothing, using a fallen tree as a barre. It was pleasant doing his exercises in such an expansive vista where he could look at the blue sky and the dense forest instead of the mirrors and walls of a studio, and he ended up shedding his outer jacket as the sun rose in the sky.

Now with no wind, the fire starts easily as soon as the flames reach the papery birch bark, and Gabriel sits down on the stump he's pulled up near the fire, and feels quite efficient as he fries his fish. He allows himself to forget its unpleasant end on the spear. The wolf dog sits comfortably nearby, as though they have sat watching fish fry many times together over the years, and Gabriel's gray socks and red wool blanket airing out over a tree branch behind them add a touch of domesticity to their campsite.

There was a Café Apollo somewhere in Greece–along the coast, though he can't quite recall where–known for their culinary greens: salads with mud-colored olives nestled in spinach leaves like displaced body organs, bright juicy tomatoes the color of this tent, and pale Swedish anchovies. He remembers the delicate endive and bib lettuce, the deep emerald green herbs and spinach–greens so remote from this white place as to seem mythical. And the soup was a rich lemon yellow, laced with pine nuts and rice. But this is better, this walleye that was swimming leisurely about below the ice fifteen minutes ago, now flaky and tender on Gabriel's fork. Definitely the freshest most delicious fish in the world, he's certain, as he squeezes more lemon juice on his salt and peppered fillet. With his morning coffee, and a slice of hearty rye, he wants nothing more. He tosses the dog a crust of his bread, and decides to call the wolf dog Shadow, because of how quietly he appeared, and how he follows him about so closely and attentively, as though he is Gabriel's guardian. He is happy having the dog around, for just the day, or for the rest of his life.

Chapter 15

There are no icicles on Greta's garage this morning; she'll have to look on the sunny side of Don's grocery store before she returns to the lake. Greta drives doggedly down the road to meet Dr. Winkle at the coffee shop for "brunch." She wants to get this over with. She'll be polite yet firm. She doesn't want to encourage him, doesn't want him to come back to Red Otter. Just be polite and firm, like Faun said. Yet she's anything but firm this morning, at least physically. She's trembling, though just a little. From the night, the odd night–how many times did she wake, thinking Gabriel was calling her? She thought he was calling from the next room, but each time she awoke she was in Faun's guest bedroom and it was quiet. No one was calling anyone. And it happened over and over, maybe 12 times, maybe 100 times. She would wake and listen, hear nothing, realize where she was, and look at the frosty window glowing from the almost full moon, then sink back into a deep sleep in the warm, fluffy, feather bed. The scene kept replaying itself over and over until morning, when she finally woke to a rosy dawn and felt so sweet and peaceful, as though she had just been kissed, even though she had been through this long night of interruptions.

Greta's morning drink is tea, and Faun's strong coffee has given Greta the jitters. She should have taken the toast with honey Faun offered. Now, she'll probably eat too much at the coffee shop and talk too much–she always does when she's nervous. Concentrate, she tells herself, and gives herself orders for the morning: eat just a little and don't talk too much, be polite, yet firm.

That must be his car. A yellow Karman Ghia, with black and white fake fur seat covers. At least she hopes they're fake. Are they supposed to resemble a Dalmatian? Holstein cows? And what is he doing with a Karman Ghia in Canada? Amazing he even made it up here. There's a "Mental Floss" bumper sticker on the back of the car, and an International Peace Garden sticker on the side window nearest Greta, which she reads as she pulls in. She was there once; on the border between Canada and North Dakota, beautiful formal gardens that flow over gently sloping hills. She had her picture taken beside a huge garden in the shape of a butterfly, fashioned entirely of yellow and white flowers. That's something they can talk about. She makes a point of looking in his car as she walks toward the coffee shop and is surprised to find the interior so clutter free–no papers, no empty pop cans, no old jackets or hats. Clean as a whistle.

Dr. Winkle is facing the door and sees Greta as soon as she comes through the coffee shop door. She says "Hi" and waves and he slides out of the booth, stands and bows, much like an opera singer taking a curtain call, or a magician ready to pull a rabbit out of his sleeve. The only other customer is Otto, who raises an eyebrow as he looks up over his Sunday *Winnipeg Sun* and whom Greta greets with a nod. She tries not to think about the town grapevine as she sits down across from Dr. Winkle.

"Yes," Willie says and smiles as he leans toward Greta, then taps the metal pot between them. "Hot water. I took the liberty of ordering it for our tea." He takes two tea bags out of his pocket and proceeds to pour steaming hot water into two white mugs. "Raspberry. Our favorite," he says and smiles again. "And you'll find a little surprise in the bottom of your cup when you're finished." He laughs a few very measured quiet laughs and pushes Greta's cup in front of her. So what will she find in the bottom of her cup–a penny? The tea leaves laced with LSD? A rabbit turd? An opal? She drinks. It's delicious. Gwendolyn brings menus and Greta orders orange juice and a blueberry muffin, which she knows are home-made, quite large, and delicious.

Dr. Winkle orders French toast and grapefruit juice, and as she expected, he does smell of Darrell, plus stale cigar, which actually helps somewhat. She finds Darrell's smell to be a combination of just plain uncleanliness, much like goat, plus a hint of leather and moldy rutabagas. She wasn't sure if Dr. Winkle would smell or not, though she thought he probably would.

She walked through a friend's snazzy new dairy barn once before going to see a play, and simply walking through the barn without touching a thing left the cow barn smell on her clothes, her hair, her skin. All evening she could smell the barn even though the dairy had glistened with new stainless steel pipes and glass tubing. It had been a cold fall day and the barn was warm with the sweet smell of cows which she didn't really mind; it was the barn smell she didn't like.

"Dr. Winkle–I hope you won't mind if I call you Dr. Winkle. I'm more comfortable with that. Is that your yellow car out front, with the–is it Holstein-patterned seat covers?"

"Yes, yes. You know your cows. Very good."

Greta's muffin arrives still warm, and she sees the outline of the big dipper in the blueberries on its sugary brown top. Dr. Winkle empties the syrup container over his pancakes, thoroughly drowning Gwendolyn's lovely buttermilk pancakes, which disgusts Greta unreasonably, and she tries not to grimace.

He says nothing as he forks soggy pancake pieces into his mouth, looking at Greta all the while with the bulging eyes of an adoring snake. Start talking Greta, do something, she tells herself. She peels the paper from her muffin and tells him she hasn't done the stained-glass work he wanted, the rabbits, that she isn't able to work on commission and simply has to do whatever comes to her.

He stops eating and looks crestfallen. "Oh," he says, as syrup drips from his fork. She tells him he's welcome to one of her recent pieces; that she has done a window for her friend Faun's outhouse, and is nearly finished with two other small windows, one round and one square. He looks happy again and his head moves in a delicate sideways motion, then slightly forward as he sops up another pancake. The cobra movements of his head and neck, along with the combination of the dirty Darrell smell and the sweet maple syrup is making Greta queasy. She holds her tea cup firmly and explains how the outhouses are emergency back-up measures because of the occasional frozen pipes.

"I've no problem with outhouses. No problem whatsoever with bodily functions," he says. "And there's no rush with the stained glass, no reason to hurry. I may be here for weeks. I've nearly convinced Darrell to take me on as an apprentice–in the art of leather decoration. Darrell's going to sleep on it and let me know in the morning. I think an art would be good for me, and he really does have the nicest tools. But I do have an ulterior motive and that is, helping Darrell with his problem. His hygiene problem. It may be he has a water problem; it may be he has a soap problem. Extreme fear of the unknown, you see. Most extreme. I plan to start with one foot. I'll have him soak the right foot in, oh, say a pail of warm soapy water, not hot water, no no. Just warm water. Pleasant, you see. Then when he discovers he can survive soap and water on the right foot, we may have him on the road to recovery. The right foot is the key to success. Did you know that?"

Greta shakes her head "no."

"But of course I won't reveal my plan to him now. I'd jeopardize my chance of getting the apprenticeship, which I'm very keen on getting." Dr. Winkle runs his forefinger around the remaining puddle on his plate, then smiles at

Greta with the sweet finger in his mouth. Greta wonders why the obscene is so fascinating, so repulsive.

She pokes tentatively at the deep red bits at the bottom of her tea cup. Perhaps some type of dried fruit. Yes, delicious tangy dried cherries, softened and warmed by the raspberry leaf tea, and she thinks it appropriate now, that he bowed like a magician when she came into the shop. A visit with Dr. Winkle is like visiting a little walking magic shop, with surprising treats and horrors, you never know what or which you'll get.

When Gwendolyn takes away their plates, Dr. Winkle hands Greta an attractive package wrapped in a tasteful dull gold paper. She opens the present cautiously. Two volumes of poetry. The top one verse by Robert Browning, and the other, poetry of Mallarmé, in French.

"One for Sunday and one for Saturday," he says, pleased with his gift.

"Next time I'll bring you some coal," he laughs, and he leans so far forward Greta fears his sleeves are on his plate. He's so pleased with every second of this brunch with Greta, with his association with her, and with himself.

Greta tries to remember what she was going to tell him, says she must get back to the lake; that she's afraid she's not a very sociable person and has work to finish, and she'll leave a stained-glass window for him, he can pick it up at Don's Grocery on Monday or Tuesday. He raises his eyebrows, and tells her one's sociability can be increased and asks if she'll join him for dinner here at the coffee shop tomorrow night. She tells him no, but agrees to meet him here next Sunday for brunch again, if he's still in town

"I'll be here. Just you wait and see," he says, as he helps her slip into her coat. Things change with Willie in town, you'll see."

As Greta drives away she doesn't notice how hard

she's clutching the steering wheel until her fingers start to tingle and her knuckles have turned pale. By the time she turns into her driveway, she's decided to drive down to Winnipeg for a few days. She tells herself she's not afraid, she's not running away, that she just needs a change of scene. She's forgotten the icicles, she forgot to look for them on the roof of Don's Grocery, and it will be the first day she's missed all month.

Several fresh deer tracks cross her front yard, nothing unusual about that, but she senses something, and walks down to her dock and looks across the expanse of White Deer Lake and listens to the silence of the Canadian winter. The white emptiness on such a sunny day usually gives her much peace and satisfaction, but today she feels an ache in her heart which she is sure has nothing to do with Dr. Winkle. She stands on the dock for a long time in the cold, waiting for something, though she doesn't know what. Inside, everything looks the same. She writes on her calendar. "I'm becoming part of snow."

Greta waters the plants, writes a note to Faun, then quickly packs. She'll stay a day or two, depending on how she feels, but she'll definitely stay over at least one night. She carefully slips the small square window into a cardboard mailer, seals it well and writes Dr. Winkle on its front with a blue felt tip pen. She packs the second, the round window, to take to Winnipeg. She'd like to find an outlet there; Thunder Bay is so far it takes all day to get there. She doesn't have the attachment to the town or Lake Superior that Faun has, and doubts she'll develop one, especially since Dr. Winkle's office is so near the art co-op.

As she's about to leave she looks back at the rooms of her cabin and wonders, as she always does when she's going farther than just into Red Otter, if she'll ever come back, if she'll ever see her cabin again. Will she ever have her sunny workroom she's so looking forward to? She lingers a moment–the winter sunbeams on the oak floor are perfectly beautiful, they always remind her of a dance studio. Today the sunbeams seem like ghosts. She shuts the door quietly, and makes two trips to the car with her suitcase and the stained-glass pieces. She hoists a heavy bag of sand from the garage into the trunk, tucks in the snow shovel, and tosses an old gray wool blanket on top of everything. Tom has started chopping wood. He usually doesn't chop on Sundays. He must be feeling better, making up for lost chopping time. She catches a glimpse of Frozi's pink winter jacket slipping through the pines and poplars, sees her stop and stand still, trying to hide behind a pine as Greta drives past.

Greta stops at Faun's mailbox, slips the note inside, and flips up the flag. She doesn't want to waste time, since the forecast is for continuing fair and sunny weather today, with colder temperatures and a possible storm moving in sometime tomorrow. She can easily make it to Winnipeg before dark if she leaves right away and makes good time. Once in town, she intentionally drives past Darrell's, spots Dr. Winkle's bright yellow Karman Ghia parked in the driveway. She wants to be sure her imagination hadn't played tricks on her, and yes, the car is as yellow-yellow as she had thought.

She leaves the stained-glass window at Don's Grocery with Mrs. Don, who says she'll give it to Dr. Winkle if he comes into the store, but she's not going out of her way to let him know it's here. Dora Don tries to warn Greta, says he's a "real odd duck." Greta readily agrees, and assures Mrs. Don that he's perfectly harmless, just a real odd duck, just as she says. She buys a package of chocolate-covered raisins, her way of measuring the distance when she drives by herself. Every ten kilometers she gets one raisin, or she waits and has three every 25 km.

On the road, by 13 raisins she's on the north edge of

Winnipeg and needs to stop for a restroom, plus she needs a drink. She spots a new store, a natural health food store, just off the road near the sign to Loon Lake. Or perhaps it isn't new, she just hadn't noticed before, but she comes to Winnipeg so seldom these days, she can't tell what's new and what's old. A big bright sign, decorated with hand-painted fruits and vegetables reads: "Northern Natural Food Store–Food for a Happy Heart and a Healthy Spirit."

They're ready to close for the day, but the two women in the store seem in no hurry and let Greta in to use the restroom and buy what she needs, at her leisure. The restroom is in a corner of the storage room; neat, tidy and smelling of sandalwood. Back in the commercial section of the store she chooses organic apple cider and an alfalfa sprout and cheese sandwich on 12 ½ grain bread while listening to the two women discuss a play about a family who live in an organic garden. She'd like to see this play, she tells them when she sets her items down on the counter, says it sounds very interesting, and asks who the playwright is. The tall lady laughs and introduces herself as Snow Bird and says she's writing the play, and she hasn't quite finished the first act, but is glad it interests Greta. The other woman is Tia, who says the apple cider is pressed from the MacIntoshes from her orchard, that each year she adds three trees to her orchard and this is her first commercial venture with the trees, and she hopes Greta enjoys it.

Greta looks over the leaflet about the moon walk while Tia rings up her purchases.

"Tomorrow night," Tia says. "It'll be a wonderful moon walk, if we beat the storm that's supposed to move in."

"I just might come," Greta tells the woman, whom she feels an immediate affinity with. She slips a flyer into her purse.

"We meet right here at 7:45, for cider, then we leave for the walk around Loon Lake at eight o'clock. Come if you can, we'd love to have you," Snow Bird calls out as Greta leaves the store.

She's been noticing the moon more as the years go by. She likes to think of it as the same moon that shone down on her as a child, that shines down now on the graves of her parents, and will someday shine above her own final resting place. Maybe Gabriel's tomb is in a cemetery in Winnipeg. She could go to a cemetery office and ask; they would give her his grave number and a map and she could wander around the cemetery grounds hunting in the snow, over hills, past markers and statues. He would be near tall birch trees covered in snow, and she would know before she saw his stone, before she saw his angel, that she had found him.

"You all right?" Tia asks, coming out of the store she's locked up behind her for the night. Greta doesn't know how long she has been sitting in the parking lot, and is startled at herself. She rolls her window down a bit. "Fine, I'm fine. Just taking a little rest before I drive into town," she says.

Tia looks into Greta's car.

"I'm not so sure. Here, you take this." She hands Greta a card. "Call me. I don't care what time it is. You just call me if you need to talk to someone."

"Thanks," Greta says to this kind woman whom she knows means exactly what she says.

Tia pats the car windshield in lieu of Greta's shoulder, then watches Greta drive out to the Winnipeg exit. Greta drives toward Winnipeg thinking of the women, the ancient moon, and just what the one-half grain in the 12 ½ grain bread might be.

Greta checks into a motel where she has stayed before, the Snow Palm, knowing she won't need a reservation at this time of year. The Snow Palm is clean, reasonable, has a restaurant, and a good-sized and well-maintained whirlpool spa. She hangs up her clothes, organizes her toiletries, and pours the apple cider into the coffee maker to heat. She throws all the pillows onto one bed, drapes a bath-size towel over the TV, and by the time she's unwrapped her sprout and cheese sandwich and kicked off her shoes, the cider is hot. Delicious. What a stroke of luck to discover the health food store. And it's comforting to know she has Tia's card in her purse—someone she could call anytime. Funny, she really could talk to Tia if she had to, if she needed to, and as friendly as she is with Faun, and they've been friends for over five years, it's this new person, Tia, she could talk to about Gabriel. Not that she will. Still, it is nice that she could.

Before she met Faun it was always hard for her to be friends with women, although she had always had women friends, and girl friends when she was a child. Yet she always felt more comfortable, more at home, with men, whether they were lovers or platonic friends. They were more straight-forward and kind she thought, less silly and jealous. There were so many jealousies back in her dancing days, and she was often the cause. Especially with Violet. Violet hated Greta's close friendship with Gabriel. In class if Gabriel chose Greta to partner him, Violet fumed. She changed color like a chameleon; her eyes darkened and her skin took on a ruddy flush. Violet was a person of extremes, not only in her jealous rages, but in her outrageous laughter, her funny pranks, her energy as a dancer. She and Violet were even friends for a time. They used to have great fun doing playful variations of their dance routines after rehearsals. Sometimes they had picnic lunches in the park near the zoo with Gabriel, and took long quiet walks along the river to listen to the birds. Violet was good at identifying several species by their song, and Greta could whistle the chirp of the robin, song sparrow, and red-winged black bird. Violet did the loon. Her loon call is the only thing Greta still remembers with any fondness. Then in the late fall, Greta and Gabriel started to avoid Violet.

Now neither Greta nor Violet dance. Violet married their first year dancing coach, the one they called "The Praying Mantis," and now she is working on a degree in business. Greta wouldn't have been at all surprised to hear Violet was in theater, if not dance, but business? That really surprised her. It was last fall when she ran into Violet outside the Winnipeg library that she heard about Gabriel. With no preliminaries, Violet came right out and told Greta that Gabriel was dead. Greta thought her heart would stop right there on the library steps. She fought back tears as they walked down the stairs and she kept saying something about how young they were and Violet talked about his headaches and she said heartaches by mistake and quickly corrected herself. Greta didn't really hear anything Violet said after that, she only heard sounds, though Violet kept talking all the way to the bottom of the stairs where she got into a cab with her briefcase. Greta remembers the finality of the cab door slamming, how it was like the closing of a coffin.

She had continued to walk along the sidewalk as if in a vacuum, until she passed someone smoking a pipe, and the sweet smell of tobacco was all she could think of. And Gabriel dead, the strong incense of pipe tobacco, and walking along the sidewalk. She kept walking, paying attention to the cement of the sidewalk, the cracks in the cement, the leaves, red maple leaves all along one block. She had stopped to look up at a particularly bright tree, a maple, on the corner before her parking lot, and stood there shaking and looking up at the branches of the tree, waiting for leaves to fall. Like a crazy person in the big city, she knew, even then, and later, thinking about it, she was afraid she had put her hands out to catch the leaves as they fell, but hoped she hadn't. She was frozen in a little shell of space that afternoon. She didn't want to live, of that she was sure, and also just as sure she would never tell anyone, not even Tia, how it was for her then, in those nightmarish long fall days.

She slips on her bathing suit, grabs the big towel off the TV and heads down the hall, walking barefoot along the red and brown carpeted hallway to the spa. Two men with big stomachs are in the water. She steps into the corner of the hot tub furthest from them. Very warm, very good. She lets her legs float out in front of her–her right knee is sore from the drive. She loves to float in the center of these bubbling pools. She'll float when the stomachs leave. They're talking about pike and walleyes. Ice fishing and rotten ice. Muskies. The man with the hairy chest is telling the bare-chested man he can keep going on a couple of suckers all winter. He threads a fine wire just under the skin–can't hit the backbone, and then he re-uses them if they don't get eaten.

Greta feels herself nearly gag at the story of sucker bait, but the hairy guy starts stretching, so she knows they'll leave soon. The bare-chested man looks at Greta, trying to think of something to say.

"We nearly sank," he says finally. "Our truck, that is. Out on Heron Lake ice fishing. Ice cracked right under us." He laughs. "Whew. Glad to to be here, I'll tell you. You from Winnipeg?" he asks Greta.

"No," she says, looking in the other direction, but still she is glad they didn't sink. She has always thought going through the ice and drowning in ice water would be the worst thing that could happen to a person.

The two stomachs talk quietly among themselves, but Greta can hear they're talking about getting a pizza and should they get sausage with snuff or rabbit and scones, it sounds like, but she knows she's not hearing right. They climb out of the tub and walk away in their soggy towels. The friendly one who told about the truck looks back and waves before disappearing around the corner. Greta steps into the center of the tub, lies back into the water, and floats in the bubbles.

Chapter 16
Night of the Full Moon

I feel sure that the surface of the Moon is not perfectly smooth, free from inequalities and exactly spherical, as a large school of philosophers considers, but that, on the contrary, it is full of inequalities, uneven, full of hollows and protuberances, just like the surface of the Earth itself.

-Galileo, The Starry Messenger, 1610

"Have you ever seen a Blue Moon?" Bobbie asks Dave.

"Seen a couple. Blue Moons, Hunter's Moon, Black Cherry Moon, Wolf Moon, Strawberry Moon–that's June. Every month's got a different name. Harvest Moon. The Blue Moon's different though. It's two moons in one month. That's not every year. You got a thing about blue?" Dave asks.

"Yah, like the bower bird. You know about the bower bird? The male collects blue things–blue feathers, string, beads, any blue stuff, bits of plastic, anything. He keeps it like an art collection. The female bower birds go for blue. Whoever has the most blue wins."

"No kidding," Dave says. "You made that up."

"No. Look it up."

"Hmm. Any in Canada?"

"Australia. I think they're in Australia."

Bobbie and Dave drive for a while thinking their respective thoughts of blue. They're about 20 km north of the health food store, where they are headed for the moon walk around Loon Lake.

"You know, we could call the CD 'Blue Barns,'"

Bobbie suggests. "Paint one of the really big barns blue, for the cover–a real tall one, or maybe find one with a blue door. Very eye-catching."

"No. It's got to be 'Ghost Barns,'" Dave says, rather hurt that Bobbie could even consider changing names. "The whole idea is ghosts you know, the ghostly wind blowing through the barns. Blue doesn't have anything to do with it."

"Oh, what the hell. I was just thinking aloud. We'll keep 'Ghost Barns.' Blue Barns is too weird anyway, I mean sick weird–not blues or jazz, anything like that–it's just weird. The more I think of it, the more it gives me the creeps. That's why you never see a blue barn." He looks over at Dave to see his reaction. "The animals would get sick," he adds.

"Hah, you're getting carried away," Dave tells him. "It's 'cause you write songs. Adding one thing and another thing, getting all worked up. That's getting into poetry. Like Dylan." But he has seen a blue barn–Maynard Mathison's, and his silo is blue too, but he won't tell Bobbie.

They're now about 10 km north of the health food store. Dave runs his finger along the top edge of the manilla envelope beside him for the umpteenth time. It contains an 8" x 10" photo of the great horned owl that lives in the woods behind his house. He took the photo at night as the owl raised his wings straight up and out, as only owls can do, and Dave thinks they look like angel wings. Out of probably more than fifty attempts, this picture turned out so good Dave could hardly believe it. He took so many shots, he couldn't figure out what he did differently that made it turn out so well. Most of the owl photos were just all dark, sometimes with a blurry white spot, or on a few the eyes showed up. He was incredulous when he developed this one; it's so professional he can still hardly believe he took it. He won't tell Tia about the bad ones.

"Deer in the ditch," Bobbie says. "Two. No three."

Dave slows down, passes them cautiously.

Bobbie sings quietly to himself, a line that's been coming to him all day.

My love is made of snow snow snow
When winter ends she melts.
At win-ter's end she melts.

He can't settle on the last line: "At winter's end she dies. When winter ends she's gone." No, "at win-ter's end she melts" –more positive. He's restless, knows this line won't let him alone until he has it right, until he's written it down, figured out the chords.

"Another sleepless night," he sighs.

"That's the full moon for you," Dave says, turning into the parking lot at the health food store.

"You sure it's okay if I come?" Bobbie asks, suddenly shy. "Since I didn't sign up or anything."

"Sure, it's fine," Dave says as he opens the door of the store and is greeted by the welcoming aroma of spiced cider and the warmth from the wood-burning stove.

Snow Bird does a subtle but noticeable double take at Bobbie and his blue Mohawk. She greets Dave warmly, and two girls in jeans, one with a blond ponytail, and the other with a long black braid down her back–they must be 9 or 10–bring cider, and offer oddly-shaped molasses cookies. Some of the cookies are small and hard looking, about the size of fifty-cent pieces, and the rest are big and lopsided, partially round with one flat edge from being placed too close together on the cookie sheet. Dave takes a small cookie and thanks the girls, figures he can dip it in the cider if it's too hard to bite.

They stand next to the stove drinking cider and Dave wonders where Tia is when he hears a car door slam. Bobbie twists the screw in his ear lobe as Snow Bird comes up to him–she's as tall as he is.

"That's infected. You ought to take that out," she says matter-of-factly. She wants to ask about his blue Mohawk, but doesn't want to seem too nosy.

"I'm in a band. A rock band," he offers. "We have to distinguish ourselves from the other groups. Otherwise we're all the same and no one can remember us. I've been thinking of getting rid of the screw."

'There's some rubbing alcohol and cotton in the back." Snow Bird starts toward the back of the store. "Come on," she calls over her shoulder. Bobbie follows.

The blond girl offers a forked tree branch to Dave. "It's a cocoon," she tells him. "We don't know what kind though. I'm hoping it's a monarch. They eat milkweed leaves."

"It's probably a mourning cloak, that's what my mom thinks," the braided girl says, peering closely at the cocoon. "Snow Bird's my mom."

Dave examines the cocoon–it looks like some of the things that grow in leftovers in the back of his refrigerator. He wishes he had his camera. He's never taken pictures of people, but he'd like to take a picture of these girls with the cocoon. He asks their names.

Snow Bird's daughter with the long braid is Tara, and the blond is Priscilla. They're in the same class at school where Snow Bird teaches third grade and Priscilla's father teachers sixth. They're in fifth grade this year, and come on the moon walks whenever it's not on a school night.

"Hi, Dave," Tia says, closing the door quietly behind her. "I thought you might come. Did you see the moon?"

"Well no. Guess I was preoccupied, but I'm ready. No sign of the storm yet."

Tia hugs Tara and Priscilla at the same time, an arm around each. Dave wants to be in the hugging group, which Tia appears to take note of. She helps herself to a cookie while Tara pours cider and Dave hands her the envelope with the owl photo. He'd like to give it to her privately, but he can't wait any longer.

"Should I open it now?" she asks.

"Yes. It's an owl," he tells her before she can slide the picture out of the envelope.

Everyone gathers around the photograph of the owl with the big eyes and great raised wings, and they all seem to like it, even Snow Bird and Bobbie, who come up behind Dave from the infirmary–Bobbie's ear lobe is covered with a small round bandage. Snow Bird says he captured the spirit of the owl, and Tia looks at Dave almost puzzled by how fine the photograph is–perhaps she doubts he took it. He tells everyone the owl lives behind his house, which he figures is proof enough that he took it.

"A great horned owl," Tara announces. "I did a report on owls last year. Everyone had to choose a different bird and I picked owls. There are 130 different kinds of owls and most of them hunt at night. They see better than we do, but when it's pitch black they find mice by hearing them move–they've got great ears. And their wings have really fluffy edges so the mice can't hear them coming. Oh I love owls," she says, looking closely at the photograph. Dave thinks she looks ready to cry.

"Somebody's here," Bobbie says, as Greta opens the door.

"Greta, come in." Tia goes to the door and welcomes her with a hug. Greta's eyes are red and puffy, but she's happy to see Tia. Greta tells Tia quietly that she doesn't want to talk much, that she's been through a crazy day but is better now and ready for the moon walk. She's had not only a crazy day but a lunatic night, yet she knows Tia understands without having to hear the details–about the bad dream of someone scratching under her bed, or under the ice–someone stuck under the ice and all alone in the cold and clawing from far away. Yet when she awoke it felt inside her, somewhere inside of her. But it didn't make sense, so Greta turned on the radio and listened to music while she waited for the night to end.

At the first hint of dawn she dressed, put on her new boots from Thunder Bay and her down parka, and drove straight to the cemetery. The snow was deep and she sank in up to her thighs and ended up sitting on the McDONALD family tombstone–its top a platform the size of her kitchen table, and the only one not completely buried under snow. She sat and watched the sunrise turn the snowy cemetery rosy pink. She didn't cry; she wasn't scared. In fact she felt safe for the first time since the scratching nightmare. When she was too cold to stay longer she plodded her way out through the snow and drove back to the motel and had a hearty breakfast. She changed, went to her favorite art gallery, to two book stores, bought glass and some new tools, and then an expensive CD player, took it all back to the motel, checked in for another day, and fell sound asleep at 1:30 in the afternoon, and it was dark when she awoke. She cried all the way to the health food store.

"It's funny, I'm all cried out and feel so calm, so peaceful," she tells Tia.

Tia takes her by the hand and makes introductions and mentions that Greta is not in a talkative mood tonight, more for Greta's sake than for any one else, since it's obvious to everyone that she has been crying and has been through some emotional turmoil. Priscilla gives Greta a cup of cider, and thinks of her mom, who is often ultra dramatic when there's a full moon.

Snow Bird looks everyone over before they leave to see if anyone needs a scarf or heavier coat and to see if their boots are adequate for snow shoeing. They keep snowshoes in the old shed at the three-quarters point of the trail, where the snow is often too deep to get through without snowshoes or skis. Up to that point, Tia and the deer keep the trail open between moon walks. Snow Bird insists that Priscilla slip on a pair of heavy gray socks that come up to her knees, and then they are ready to start.

Tara and Priscilla lead, sprinting ahead and darting back to the grownups, much in the manner of frisky pups. It's cold and the night is bright with moonlight. After a quarter of a mile the girls' excess energy has slowed them to the pace of the adults, and the moon's magic has put them in a mood. At the front of the trail; the girls chant:

"Star bright, star light,
first star I see tonight,
I wish I may, I wish I might,
have the wish I make tonight."

"You know my wish?" Dave asks Tia. "I want you back." He goes on without giving her time to respond. "I'm much more interesting now than I used to be, thanks to the camera. Tia, I see so much more now. I'm like a walking camera–very receptive–I'm always noticing things. Like the moon on your shiny blue parka. Aren't we going to stop?"

"We stop just around the corner up ahead, at Look Out Point," Tia says. Dave is sure she sounds friendlier than she has for a long time, and he sighs wistfully.

Behind the girls, Bobbie has been questioning Greta.

"No. She said 'ballet dance,' not 'belly dancing,'" Snow Bird tells Bobbie. "Isn't that right Greta?"

"Yes, ballet," Greta says, in a near whisper. Dave thinks of Gabriel, but he's the last one on the trail and too far behind to tell Greta about his ballet dancer friend. He doesn't want to shout. Anyway, if he said something, he's sure Tia would remind him Greta doesn't feel like talking. He doesn't want Tia mad at him.

Snow Bird passes Bobbie in order to be between he and Greta, so he won't bother her with more questions.

They're nearly to Look Out Point. Snow Bird starts talking to distract the conversation away from Greta, whom she saw literally jump when Bobbie started questioning her.

"Well, my husband met his end in these woods," Snow Bird says. "Or rather the beginning of his end. He was a logger, and he lost his grip somehow, and the chain saw flipped out of his hand and cut his arm clean off—he fell on top of the thing. We thought he'd make it for a while, but he'd lost too much blood. He went real fast," she says. She doesn't mention how he carried his own arm out of the woods like a bloody dripping log.

Tara comes and holds her mother's hand. She's heard her mother tell this story a thousand times. They've talked about it and decided she should tell the story whenever she needs to, that it's better to tell it, than to think it, or dream it. Before, her mother had chain saw nightmares all the time. Tara was too little to even remember her dad, so the story has never seemed quite real to her, but she adores her mother. Someday Tara is going to be a psychologist. She's recently decided; it's in her genes, she's sure. Her great grandfather was a famous medicine man, and she's very proud of him, even though he died way before she was even born.

"You should try a braid, like Tara's," Snow Bird tells Bobbie, as she takes the end of Tara's braid, which slides through her fingers as Tara skips ahead to join Priscilla. "That blue dye isn't good. Who all's in your band?"

"Oh, there's Lila on sax. Her hair is pink—very short, and real fine, like baby hair. She says she uses fabric softener on it, but you can't believe her. She lives on drugs and grapefruit. She sings too. Closes her eyes and sings, but it's more like a high whistle than singing, a kind of whistle-humming really. You might think of a bird. She becomes an instrument. She shakes her head and shoulders and does echoes with the microphone. You'd have to hear her. You can't hear her though, because we're mostly just noise," Bobbie says, with a laugh that breaks with regret in the cold air.

"Then there's Point on guitar. He's an actor, unfortunately for us, at least this year. We've had to turn down gigs because of it. He's in a musical version of "The Lost Ones" at the Ice House Theater through next weekend. He got Lila in on that one. She has a recurring solo, which some people call a recurring nightmare. Beckett, you know. But Point's really good. He's bald and has his head tattooed with Zodiac signs."

"Veggie's on bass. A perfectly normal guy, maybe a little too healthy looking. Definitely too good looking for his own good. The girls are always after him."

"Maybe you're jealous?" Snow Bird suggests.

"Sure. Definitely. I envy his energy anyway. The guy never stops."

"Vegetarian?"

"Yah, he doesn't make a big deal of it though," Bobbie says. "and last there's Tom on percussion. Lila's boyfriend who never talks. Quietest person I've ever met."

"So Lila, who sort of sings and sort of whistles, is your singer?" Snow Bird asks.

Bobbie hesitates, then says he's the singer, as well as keyboardist.

Snow Bird is intrigued with Bobbie, and finds his outward appearance unreflective of his inner self. She has a feeling he probably sings the most soulful German lieder. She already knows he has heart-breaking eyes and sensitive earlobes.

At Look Out Point two old willow branches jut out over the lake offering their thick branches as front row seats, or "pews," as Priscilla's dad calls them. He's home with a cold, she tells everyone, as she slides her legs over the willow and sits down. Bobbie comes up behind her and traces a circle on her back, and says:

"Draw a magic circle,
line it with purple,
put in the eyes,
put in the nose,
but who put in the mouth?"

She giggles. "You Bobbie."

"No, I only did the eyes and the nose."

"Me," Tia says and gives Priscilla's ponytail a playful tug. They all settle down on the branches, legs dangling above the lake, except for Bobbie and Snow Bird and Dave, whose legs reach the ground. When Priscilla's dad is along, she tells them, he imitates a train whistle, and asks everyone for their ticket and calls out "Last call for the moon." Priscilla loves when he's silly like that, even though she pretends to be embarrassed. "The moon is perfectly round again this month," he sometimes says. And it is, so round, so perfect. She knows long ago they used to think it was made out of a kind of crystal, with a big fire inside. Personally it makes her think of fire flies–it has that kind of glow to it; it's not like an ordinary light at all.

Dave studies the moon for the kind of cheese it most resembles, and settles on Swiss.

"Maybe I'll never see a full moon again," Greta says to Snow Bird, who is sitting beside her. "Not like this anyway," she adds. "It's so beautiful."

"Every moon is different," Snow Bird says. Shh," she points down the lake. A dozen deer are at the lake's edge, just 30 feet ahead of them. The moon shows up the white of their ears, and they are so close Greta can almost feel the texture of their fur. The closest male turns toward them, pausing for a moment as the light glistens on his antlers, and then with great dignity, he steps away, and one by one the deer leap up the snow bank and disappear into the trees.

"Can you imagine living in the woods all your life, and

never going inside?" Tara asks. "I hope they're happy."

"They are," Snow Bird says.

"As long as the wolves stay away," Dave says, then wishes he hadn't said anything, that he didn't have such a big mouth. He gently bounces on the willow bough, embarrassed, trying to rock-a-bye, trying to sooth everyone.

"If I were a wolf, I'd sing to a moon like this one," Bobbie says, wondering where the moon has been all these years–thinks he's only seen it in movies and hasn't really seen it since he was a kid.

"They howl, I don't think they sing," Dave says.

"Both," Snow Bird says. "They howl and they sing. The howling is a type of song. What kind of songs do you do Bobbie, in your group?"

"Hard Rock. Loud. You really can't hear us. Like I said, we're mostly noise, I'm afraid. My background is classical though." He's surprised at his own confession. He hardly ever tells anyone about his background. "I'd like to listen to Bach out here. It seems so spiritual with the moon so close, and it's amazingly quiet. Man, this sky really gets me. You guys do this every month?"

"Yes, unless the weather's really bad. In fact, I didn't think we'd be out here tonight. They predicted a storm," Tia says.

"Do you know Glen Gould's *Goldberg Variations?*" Greta asks Bobbie.

"God, yes. What genius. Bach and Gould." He leans over and smiles at Greta. "My grandfather heard Gould play–once in Toronto, and the last time in Winnipeg."

"An old friend of mine, well, his father, was a friend of Gould's" Greta says. "It's too bad he died so young."

Snow Bird says they'd better move along, they'll probably have some snowshoeing up ahead, and that will slow them down.

"I feel the storm coming. I feel it in my knees," Dave says.

"I feel it in my right knee," Greta laughs. "Our premonitions are in our bones."

"That's true," Snow Bird says. "People have their experiences through their injuries now days. But humans and animals used to be more in touch with the earth. It's well known that animals sense earthquakes beforehand. We were all like that once. In touch with the elements, and with all creatures. Our bodies had a natural intelligence. Most everyone has lost that sensitivity, or they ignore it or don't even recognize it when it comes to them."

Greta wonders if Snow Bird knew about her husband's accident ahead of time, and if she did, what good is it to know if you can't do anything to prevent it. She worries about the vague things she senses, and is thankful for their vagueness. They walk along single file without speaking, moving rapidly along the narrow path. Their eyes are adjusted to the bright black and white of moonlight, and they walk in the night's negative light, sensitized by the moon, developing under the light of the moon. The only sound is the crunching of snow, and their cold quick breathing, until they hear the howl of a wolf in the distance, its cry muffled by thick conifer forest, and Greta feels her hair stand on end.

At the shed Tara tests the trail. The snow is deep; they'll need snowshoes. Bobbie is the only one who's never used snowshoes, so Snow Bird helps him strap up and demonstrates how best to walk. Dave breaks the trail, which is dusted with new snow glittering like stars, above a crusty under layer and several feet of loose deep snow.

The birch trees are so white and bright Dave thinks they look like fake Hollywood trees, but he keeps the thought to himself. They walk silently and use their energy to move as quickly as their snowshoes allow them to go. The wind has started up and they're racing the storm.

Bobbie is tired but keeps going, mesmerized by the sound of the 14 wood and rawhide snowshoes crunching rhythmically through the snow. He tries to give the sound a key, tries to think of what it reminds him of, but it's a completely new sound–a snow chord. Creaking floor boards? No, he doesn't know what, but he's decided to let his hair go normal. It would take years for it to get long enough to braid. He wonders if everyone feels this icy cold in their lungs. As they turn a corner he spots the light of the store, about 300 yards ahead, and Tara and Priscilla shout out "Hooray, we made it" in unison and Tia says her lungs need defrosting.

Bobbie hears Dave, though he knows he's not suppose to hear, tell Tia he'll be glad to help her defrost, and Bobbie hopes he will. There's something about the moon that binds people, he's decided. He really feels close to all these people, especially Snow Bird, and he only knew Dave before.

Greta keeps thinking she's almost not here, but it's okay. How perfectly crazy and wonderful. She has a good feeling about the future. And they're at the store at last. Before going inside, Greta starts her car, and lets it run to warm up, then takes the stained-class window inside and gives it to Tia, who's standing next to the wood-burning stove.

"You can put this in your front window," Greta tells her.

"Greta, thanks! It's beautiful." Tia kisses Greta's icy cheek.

At the door, Priscilla hands Snow Bird her shoes. "Crows go south, usually, and ravens stay here," she ways. "We're ravens. I did crows and ravens for my report last year." She suddenly imitates the cry of a crow, then puts her hand over her mouth, both surprised and delighted with herself, and unable to decide whether she prefers crows or ravens.

"Well, that's a good note to end the night on," Tia

says. "Thanks for coming everyone. Take care getting home. Hope you can all come next month."

Dave tells Bobbie he won't need a ride home, that he should go on into Winnipeg and he'll call him in the morning.

Greta pauses at the door. "Tia, what's the one-half grain? In the 12 ½ grain bread?

"Oh that. Wild rice. Night now."

Chapter 17

Curled up in his den, the snow is burying him. The pine boughs are soft, he can smell the pine. Gabriel doesn't mind the wind, and rather likes the sound, the roar. It seems like the world is blowing away, tumbling through the woods. He thought his feet were cold but now he's warm, almost hot. His balance isn't right–he's too heavy on one side, toward the ground, but he's holding on. Tries not to tip over. But he's lying down. *Petrouska,* second act. Very heavy sleep until the snow on his eyes wakes him. Impossible to change but he must try to do *Giselle* with these strings but the music is wrong. Stravinsky. It's too hot, his feet are on fire. How wet. You're pushing me, no let me sleep. No, no. Gabriel pushes Shadow away, but he persists and continues to lick Gabriel's face, pawing at his shoulder, until Gabriel opens his eyes and sees the wolf dog standing before him with his unfathomable eyes.

"Oh God," he moans and tries to stretch his legs.

Dr. Saunier's Meditation

He saves his best Japanese incense for the night of the full moon, and its subtle perfume, along with the sweet birch of the wood-burning stove, and a hint of green tea, create an irresistible invitation to the spirit.

Dr. Saunier is seated in lotus position in the center of his meditation room and has been in deep meditation for nearly two hours. After tea, he slipped on his white robe and seated himself where he could see the full moon through his round garden window, which is placed to frame the rising moon. He chanted for Gabriel before allowing his eyes to sink, before entering his center, where the image and thoughts of the world drift away like clouds and he becomes part of the cosmos, unruffled by the great white Canadian storm around him and effortlessly, he directs energy and light toward Gabriel.

———————

Carl Come-so-Far's phone is still busy when Latos tries for a second time to get through. Out the window the blizzard rages and snow has curtained the windows so Latos sees out through a small opening in the center of the pane. Snow has drifted back up against the lodge door and he'll have to plow the drive again when he goes out to check on the dogs. Looking out the little peephole in the center of the snowy window seems like looking into an old-time black and white photograph, all white and cold, and the shrieking of the wind makes him sad. His wife used to turn the jukebox on, turned up as loud as it would go, when they had these storms, and she would make big pots of soup. She hated winter storms. Latos loves the smell of vegetable soup cooking on a winter day and decides to make a pot to cheer himself.

In the kitchen the howling wind isn't so noticeable. Potatoes, carrots, celery, one big red onion. Half a rutabaga, which he peels. He doesn't peel the other vegetables, just chops them up into large chunks and covers it all with water. When it's done he'll fork out the celery leaves and onion skins that float to the top. She's probably bowling, he tells himself; it's all he allows himself to imagine of her. He pictures her in a kind of eternal bowling alley where everyone stomps around in clunky bowling shoes, smoking cigarettes and drinking beer, while sending bowling balls thundering down the lanes to crack the pins to smithereens.

The only time he ever went bowling was down in Winnipeg at a two-lane bowling alley where they had a pin boy in the back to set up the pins. But he's seen the modern lanes on TV–the twenty laners with automatic pin setters. Obsessively, he used to watch every weekend, that first year after she left, watching for her, watching for him. He would plan all his chores around the two o'clock Sunday bowling show, until one Sunday late in the fall when he was out fishing down by Sad Man Falls and the fishing was so good–the walleyes were practically jumping into his boat, and he completely forgot about the bowling. After that he just didn't watch anymore.

He leaves the soup to simmer and tries the phone again. Carl answers on the third ring, surprised to hear from Latos. Carl says they're all fine but a big pine fell on his boathouse, though it didn't hurt the boat any, and he and Angela are just sitting around waiting out the storm. He's sure Jim and them are fine he tells Latos, but is surprised to hear someone is camped out at Turtle Bay at this time of year, and says sure, he and Jim'll go down and see if the guy is all right.

There is a silence on the line while Jim thinks about whether to go now or wait until they can get out better, when the storm lets up. Jim's pet crow, Blackie, jumps up on the telephone table, shakes the black coils of the telephone cord until Carl scoots him away.

"Who's camping there?" Carl asks.

Latos is embarrassed that he doesn't know, that he never stopped.

"A dancer," he says.

"Oh. I'll go get Jim," he says. "We'll get em."

Carl hangs up abruptly, his mind already planning. He packs the scant number of items he considers essential survival supplies. He dresses in fur. His sister prepares his food: nuts and dried elk, flat-bread, a skin flask of water. Blackie flies to the porch and watches Carl lace his boots from his antler perch above the kerosene lantern. Carl straps on his snowshoes and pack, tells Angela he'll be fine, clicks his tongue at Blackie and leaves the warm cabin.

He decides to go through the woods, where he'll have some protection from the fierce winds. The blizzard roars above the tree tops, yet it's quiet near the ground. Carl moves swiftly over the deep snow, zigzagging his way toward Jim Nightman's. He follows the ridges of bushy spruce and jack pine to the frozen river, then moves along the protected side by Hawk Ridge, to where it meets the lower deer trail that will take him to potato patch, the small meadow behind Jim's cabin. He knows the way so well he could walk to Jim's in his sleep, or on a moonless night, which indeed, he has done a time or to.

The temperature has fallen and Carl takes long deep breaths and concentrates on the warmth of his breath and the heat of his blood, to keep himself warm, and the thought of the dancer helps him keep up his pace. They used to dance, his people did. His nephew, Ottaway, tells him they still do–down in South Dakota where Ottaway has lived since he turned 18. He knows the old language, the old arts–makes moccasins, skin shirts–he hears all about South Dakota when Ottaway comes back each December. But Carl couldn't live there. Life without the lake would be no life at all.

At the edge of the meadow there is an odd mound of snow. Coming closer, Carl sees a great moose antler curve up out of the snow. He breaks a branch and approaches. He pokes at the dead moose, which is stiff but not yet frozen, and he brushes the snow away from its face and says the old words for the spirit of the moose. Perfect snow crystals have formed along the black nostrils, shaped from its last breath. A better death, in winter, Carl feels. No flies, no worms, just a blanket of snow. He and Jim can get him later, after they find the dancer. Carl hopes they won't find the dancer dead like this.

"Carl," Jim says, holding the door open. Carl leaves his snowshoes on the porch and tells Jim about the call from Latos, and about the camper down at Turtle Bay. He warms himself by the fire, holding out his hands, taking off his boots to warm his cold feet while Jim gets ready. When he puts his boots back on, Jim mentions the moose back in the meadow.

"Oh," Jim says. "that must've been what Shadow was fussing over, pulling at my pants leg, trying to get me out for something, last night. That wolf dog, you know, that Latos gave me."

"He's a dear," Sara Blue says. "So nice, and smart too," she smiles, crazy about the dog, and not at all worried like Jim is, about him being out in the blizzard.

"He ain't froze yet," Carl says. "The moose."

"No," Jim says as he buttons his parka. "Well, I bet you anything it's that lame moose we saw last fall. He's been around lately, eating the hay by the root cellar. It's a miracle the wolves never got him.

"They'll be after him soon as the storm lets up," Carl says. "We'll get him when we get back," Jim tells Sara Blue, and they head off together toward Turtle Bay, which they need to reach before the sun sets, which is still early in January.

Sara Blue watches the men walk past the fallen pine and disappear into the blizzard, where they'll follow the lake's edge all the way to the bay. She pours herself a cup of herb tea and settles herself beside the stove, ready to take up where she left off with her bead work; no more concerned about the men than about the wolf dog. Not worried at all; quite content to be a woman, and not a man or a dog.

Over at Dave's house, Tia finds Gabriel's note to Dave when she sweeps the crumbs, socks, and candy wrappers out from under his kitchen table. Dave is in the shower singing–probably Bob Dylan's "Hard Rain's Gonna Fall," his favorite shower song, which she knows from past experience and his love of routine-certainly not from what she hears. His voice is strictly a monotone with no range whatsoever–the spray of the shower has a wider range. The note from Gabriel isn't dated, but it couldn't be too old since it's written on the back of her most recent moon walk notice. Tia hopes Gabriel is back from this outdoor trip by now, certainly he wouldn't be out in this storm. Even in Dave's big truck with the plow they had some rough going driving to Dave's this morning, and the storm is not supposed to let up for another twenty-four hours. She and Dave talked about asking Gabriel to the next moon walk. She's pretty sure he and Greta would have a lot in common.

She's mopped the floor and is re-reading Gabriel's note when Dave comes bouncing down the stairs, pink and happy and smelling of soap. He comes up behind Tia and puts his arms around her and reads the note from Gabriel over her shoulder.

"Dave, you're pinching me," Tia nearly yelps. His reaction to the note has tensed his entire clean body; he's horrified he hadn't seen the note before. How could he have missed it? He sits down at the kitchen table and dials Gabriel's number. He gets the answering machine–no voice, just some piano music and someone humming. He hangs up. The studio. No, of course not. No phone there.

Chapter 18
The White Place

Without a body, the snow is neither hot nor cold and the history of each snowflake is more easily perceived and sifted in the slow white rhythm of the cosmic heart. Gabriel cannot tell himself from the music of the snow. The cavern of his ears fill with swirling white until the rubbing, the rubbery wet rubbing opens his eyes to the dog in the snow, licking him awake. He can't do that again, can't stop to rest, can't fall, can't sleep.

Shadow tugs at his parka until he gets to his knees. Stands. Wobbly as a marionette, his feet move as independent entities; his knees lift abnormally high, they jerk. But he moves. He follows Shadow into the night of snow. North, south, east, west, all the same. He moves through the snow with his body of air, in and out, in and out. He breathes the snow, he breathes life into himself, back into his body, his limbs again coordinate, he senses himself entering his musculature. Muscles, tendon, bone. Flowing blood, hot skin, his spine alive, and he glides through the snow like an animal, like a bird, like Gabriel. A dancer again.

Shadow watches, then quickens his pace. Gabriel keeps up. All Gabriel can think is: traveling through sky, through spirit. He knows the snow is his final home, always there, waiting for him. The snow is pure spirit.

The orange flag. Two men in parkas, looking at him with their eyes, their dark eyes. Waving. He can't remember what to do. What part does he have? He's forgotten. The last thing he hears is a motor, the last thing he sees before he falls is Shadow, his eyes like stars, guiding him. He doesn't mind; he's home.

Three Days Later:

Gabriel is asleep in his hospital room, while Greta sits in a chair at the head of the bed. As the late afternoon sun moves across his forehead, Gabriel stirs and opens his eyes.

"Hello," Greta says.

He reaches out to her her - their hands are warm. The lost years slip away.

Northern Goose Photo Shop
6 mm/DVD conversion

La vie de Gabriel Dimetri Perez
Danser de Ballet Extraordinaire

Directeur/Montage - Juliette Dubois

Winnipeg: Home movie. Acrobatic stunts in back yard. Mother wearing large black hat, waves from porch.

Barcelona: Still shot of Gabriel as a child, 7 years old, standing on park bench in Guadi Park.

Montreal: Morning class–at the barre.

London: Opening night, *Theme and Variations*, and after performance reception.

Paris: Dress rehearsal–*Giselle.*

Copenhagen: Walking along the shore, skipping rocks with friends.

New York: "Dear Petrouska" –Gabriel in bluejeans–clowning in Central Park.

Winnipeg: Rehearsal for *Apollo.* Gabriel and Greta in white.

Gabriel looks to the camera. Fade out.

FIN